The Black Sisterhood Files

Kristina Naydonova

ISBN: 9798615455865

Contents

ACKNOWLEDGMENTS

Dedicated to my loving and supportive family: my sister, Sophia; my mother, Anna; and my father, Oleg. Thank you for providing me with so much care, guidance, and exciting opportunities. This book is devoted to you. I love you forever.

Thank you as well to Daniel Pink, Michelle Hillier, and many more for being my mentors throughout this journey. I greatly appreciate your insights and time.

CHAPTER ONE

A steady murmur spread throughout the hallways of Parkersburg High. I stood at the beginning of the hallway, clutching my books close to my chest. Everyone passed by me, chattering and giving me odd looks. My younger sister, Carly, stood sorrowfully by her jammed locker, trying to flag a teacher down.

It was our first day in Parkersburg, West Virginia and our first day at Parkersburg High School. Back in Pennsylvania, Mom and Dad had trouble with paying rent and we were forced to move into a one-room apartment without a bed. I spent nights pretending to be asleep on our mattress, while I listened to Mom cry and Dad quietly talk with someone over the phone.

The move happened so quickly, I barely had time to settle down and soak in my new surroundings. I tried calling all my friends back in Pennsylvania, but they were no longer interested in talking to me, blaming the move on me.

Parkersburg was a strange, but fairly small town. It was a five minute walk from my house to the new cafe where Mom worked. I didn't know anything about Dad's new job, except for the fact that it was supposed to keep our family financially stable for years to come.

As I struggled with falling asleep last night, a few very odd things happened. I had stood up from my bed to look out the window, noticing a large and clearly abandoned house, eerily perched across from my home on an unkempt lawn. It may have just been my imagination, but I could've sworn I saw someone standing by it.

"Excuse me," said a steady voice, "Excuse me." I snapped out of my train of thoughts to find a girl my age, standing in front of me. Her hair was curly brown with streaks of purple in it; long coffin earrings hung from the ends of her elvish ears.

"Uh, hi," I said, "Sorry if I was in your way. Er, I'm Lexie Torres, I'm new here."

"I figured," said the girl, a smirk on her olive colored face, "I just wanted to see if you needed any help with finding your classroom."

"I'm quite alright," I snapped irritably and pushed past the girl.

I wouldn't talk to me like that if I were you," the girl said, a hint of menace in her voice.

"Yeah, yeah, yeah," I said, rounded the corner and stopped, looking down at my schedule with anger. I realized that I was lost and didn't know where to find Classroom 203. As if she could read my mind, the same girl rounded the corner and said:

"Go straight down the hallway and turn right to get to Classroom 203."

"Thanks," I grunted and proceeded down the hallway, tripping over my feet.

"I'll see you later, Lexie," said the girl. "My name's Sophia by the way."

I ignored her and quickly rushed into my first class, receiving dirty looks from classmates and the teacher. As I sat down at my desk, apologizing hastily, I couldn't shrug off the fact that there was something very wrong with Sophia.

The rest of the day passed in a blur of teachers yelling and students laughing. Carly and I waited in the cafeteria for Mom to pick us up. Carly removed a thick binder from her backpack and got to work on homework. I lay my head down on the table, eyes fluttering shut, tired from my lack of sleep.

"Have you made any friends?" asked Carly, and I shook my head in response, "I actually met these really nice twins, Jasmine and Trinity. We might hang out soon."

"I don't care, Carly," I said, and Carly rolled her eyes. My phone vibrated and I opened it to find a text from Mom saying: "I'll be at the school in about five minutes".

"Mom's almost here," I announced, putting my phone on the cafeteria table. Carly ignored me, her face covered by a curtain of hair. I punched her lightly in the arm and turned around, feeling slightly sick. Today had been a horrible day, and I still couldn't forget Sophia.

I watched as a group of five girls entered the cafeteria, one of them holding a piece of paper. They all sat down at a table and crowded around the piece of paper, their hair providing a shield for whatever secrets they were hiding.

"Are you sure it's the right thing to do, Sophia?" one of the girls asked. Their faces were out of sight to me, but I could clearly hear everything they said. Sophia. It was the girl from this morning.

"Absolutely," said another girl, "Remember the motto of the Black Sisterhood: Differences are accepted, but failure is not."

"Is she the right person?" asked a different girl, and I sensed a hint of worry judging by the tone of her voice, "We don't want what happened with Esma to happen with her."

"Nothing like that will ever happen again," a voice that had previously spoken said. Their tone was sharp and uncompromising, bringing a sense of brutality with it.

"Yeah, Sophia' right, Ella," said yet another voice, "We've learned from our mistakes so we won't repeat them. What happened with Esma was an accident. We didn't mean for her to die."

"It wasn't our fault," one of them said in a hushed voice. I strained my ears to hear, heart pounding in my throat.

"Maybe it was a little bit, another girl murmured, "She got too stressed during Task Three. She might have chosen fears that were *too* difficult for her to fight off. I remember that night ever so clearly. Right after Task Three, Esma fled out of the studio and never came back. She was found dead at the bottom of Chthonic Cliff days later."

"Poor thing," a girl mumbled, her voice quivering, "It really must be our fault."

"Hush," suddenly said one of them, leaning in. She threw me a furtive glance and whispered something to the group of girls surrounding her. They all picked up their bags and scurried out of the cafeteria, as silent as mice.

"Mom's here, Carly," I said as my phone vibrated with a text message in the back of my backpack, "She's waiting for us by the football field."

Carly soundlessly followed me out the door, tilting her head to see a worksheet she was clutching underneath her arm. I watched her grab a pencil and scrawl something on the worksheet, scrunching up her face in confusion.

As Carly and I approached the football field, Carly still hastily doing her homework, I spotted Mom leaning on our car, talking to a tall man in skinny jeans. Carly didn't seem to notice as I pulled her behind a bush. She kept writing away at her assignment, oblivious to what was happening.

"I'm telling you, Albert, I never wanted to move here," Mom was saying, fluttering her eyelashes.

"Well, you're lucky you found me," said the man, grazing Mom's shoulder with his right arm, "My son goes to Parkersburg High as well."

"Oh, really?" asked Mom, stroking a stubble on the man's chin, "Why, that's lovely. What's his name, Albert, dear?"

"Ah, that's not important," said Albert, "Aha, we did agree that if I was to continue seeing you, I would have to pay you for the trouble this may submerge your family in. Right, dear?"

"Yes," said Mom, clamping her palms into Albert's. I observed as he slipped thirty dollars into her outstretched hands, and leaned over to kiss her on the cheek. Mom blushed and stuffed the money into the pockets of her sweatpants.

"Lucky for me, you're divorced," she said, waving the man off, "See you tomorrow, Albert." The man gave Mom an affectionate smile as he began walking down the pavement, the bare trees swaying above his nearly bald head.

Carly had looked up from her homework, and was silently watching the man with a grim countenance. Quite a few things had become manifest during these minutes of our life, which I'm sorry to say, were not the last of Albert Carly and I would see.

When you're trying to hide a particular something, you'll notice that time passes by with the speed of a hummingbird's moving wings. Carly and I tried desperately to keep our mouths shut during the ride home, and sped up to our rooms after we had arrived, using homework as an acceptable excuse.

Albert. The name kept popping up in my head again and again, and the memory of him kissing Mom on the cheek stuck like glue. Night soon swallowed the town of Parkersburg, leaving me with a deep pit of sorrow and misfortune in my stomach.

Hungry and tired, I laid down on my bed, gazing up at the moonlight reflecting off of the many windows in my bedroom. At around ten o'clock, I heard a soft knock on my door which I supposed was Mom coming to say goodnight.

"Lexie," a light voice said, "It's me. I haven't really gotten a chance to talk to you today, but I suppose we're all exhausted. Goodnight, dear. I'll see you in the morning."

I didn't answer and listened as Mom made her way to Carly's room, also knocking mellowly on her door. My eyes soon became heavy and I fell into a troubled sleep, waking up often and clutching my nightstand with clammy hands.

The clock read three o'clock in the morning when I heard the two voices. I crept out of bed and up to the window, resuming the same position as last night. The night was darker then yesterday, and I could only make out the faint outline of the two figures. One sat on the ground and it appeared to be looking up at the other figure who towered above it.

"Yes," said the terrifying voice of the taller figure, "You're right. The *person* is dead, but the *other* is not. You *saw* me as you circled *it*. I *knew* you did, which is why I *took* you."

"I understand," the other voice quivered, and buried its head into the black cloak that covered its body, "You knew I didn't want to do it, so you preyed upon me like a hawk. Braveheart and Merciless will know about this."

"Will they, though?" said the taller figure as the shorter one ran off into the forest. It stood there, dripping wet with the rain falling from the sky. And just as a rumble of thunder and a streak of lightning tore through the clouds, the creature laughed a horrible, wheezing laugh that told me something at once: my stay at Parkersburg would be unforgettable.

CHAPTER TWO

Esma. Albert. Braveheart. Merciless. Four names
that made no sense, that had appeared out of
nowhere, and that haunted me in my worst
nightmares. When the first rays of sunlight broke
through the morning clouds, I found myself hunched
over the toilet, sobbing into the toilet water.

Before long, Mom's hands were on my
shoulders, her voice filling my pounding head. Out
of the corner of my eye, I saw her close the
bathroom door and lean over me, looking
inexplicably worried.

"Lexie," she whispered, "Lexie, are you alright?
Lexie, talk to me."

"W-w-when are we going back home?" I asked,
gasping for breath and choking on the words I so
desperately wished I didn't have to ask.

"Now, now, Lexie," said Mom, "You have to
understand that Dad and I barely escaped
Pennsylvania. We owed so much debt to our
landlord and struggled with paying off taxes. Now

that your father is earning a few thousand dollars a day, I don't see a reason to complain."

"Well, I do," I gasped, wiping my eyes with the sleeve of my night clothes, "Braveheart, Esma, Merciless, and someone you know very well. These people, these people will haunt me for the rest of my life."

"Lexie, I haven't the faintest idea of what you're talking about," said Mom, standing up, "Bad dreams?"

"So much more than that," I mumbled, resting my head against the cool walls of the bathroom, "It's so much more than just a bad dream."

"I'm very sorry to hear that," said Mom, "And though I don't know what you mean, we'd better get some food in you. I'm sure you're very hungry. And aren't you cold sitting on that floor?"

"No," I replied, averting my eyes. Mom hovered over me with a helpless demeanor, sighing and rubbing my shoulders every now and then.

"I'm going to go wake Carly up and make breakfast," she finally announced, patting my head, "You had better get up soon or you'll be late for the bus. Dad and I don't have time to drive you to school."

"Mom?" I asked, looking up at my mother with wet, woeful eyes, "Is Parkersburg our permanent home?"

Mom smiled somberly and kneeled down on the floor beside me, "Even if it is," she said, taking my hand and placing it into hers, "You have nothing to worry about. Parkersburg is safe and a good social environment for all of us. Now, do tell Lexie, do you need help with anything? Is there anything, other than these nonsensical names, that is bothering you?"

Of course there was. And it wasn't just the names. The very thought of a girl named Esma throwing herself off a cliff, only to be found dead days later, chilled me to the core. And Sophia, oh that dire Sophia had something to do with it. I struggled not to let everything spill out of me at once, and bent my head down to look at the ground. I needed reassurance that everything would be alright, but Mom wasn't the person to ask for that. I needed a friend or at least an amiable person who didn't snicker or whisper something vile whenever they saw me.

"No," I fibbed, avoiding eye contact, "Everything's alright. You're right, I probably just had a bad dream. It's nothing to worry about."

"Thank you, Lexie," mumbled Mom, leaning in close to my face, "For not being silly. Enough with Braveheart, Merciless, and Esma, whoever they may be. Go get ready for school."

"Okay," I mumbled and crept past Mom to open the bathroom door. Carly was fixing herself a bagel in the kitchen while Dad stood in the hallway, whispering into his phone with a hand over his mouth.

"Oh relax, Bill," he said anxiously, "No, no, hear me out. I know Rick doesn't want me, you know, doing it with his aunt, but Boss agrees I'm the best for the night job. I don't care that Rick respects his aunt that much, she has every right to have a job like this."

"Good morning, Dad," I said, "I didn't see you at all yesterday. Why'd you have to come in so early?"

"Now, now, Alexis, does that matter concern you?" questioned Dad, straightening his tie, "I understand you're curious, but leave it to the adults to handle. I have to go to work, so see you some other time."

"Wow," I mumbled, watching as Dad grinned at his reflection in the mirror, hardly acknowledging my presence. He grabbed an apple lying on the counter and hurried out the door, struggling to carry his hefty suitcase.

"Hi, Lex,"said Carly who was sitting on the stairs, "How'd you sleep?"

"Fine," I remarked, "Just a random question, did you hear anything strange tonight?"

"No, but I heard you bawling by the toilet," snickered Carly, seemingly unbothered by the sudden interrogation. "Actually, I did hear voices. It sounded like more than two people. I was floating in and out of dreams, so I couldn't pay much attention to it, but I heard a lot of names."

"What names?" I asked, sucking in some air, my heart practically pounding out of my chest.

"Oh, I don't know," said Carly, gazing up at the ceiling as if the names she was looking for were written up there, "I think it was Blackheart and

Merciful. It doesn't matter, because I'm the only one who heard it. It was probably just a dream."

"Yeah," I said, swallowing the huge lump forming in my throat, "Of course it was just a dream. I'm not the only one who's worried about Dad's odd behavior, am I?"

"No," mumbled Carly, her eyes welling up with tears, "I came down to the kitchen this morning and he was standing there, talking to somebody on the phone. I tried to give him a hug but he just rolled his eyes and pushed me away."

"That's harsh," I said, stroking Carly's hair, "He didn't see me at all yesterday and barely even acknowledged my presence just now. It's a bit off. I remember one time Dad didn't see me for a few weeks and acted as if we hadn't seen each other in a year when he got back home. It isn't like him to act this way."

"Yeah," sighed Carly as we began descending the stairs. Carly paused at the fruit bowl to grab two persimmons and juggled the two fruits, throwing me one as the other soared through the air.

"Off to school," I said, biting into the juicy flesh of the persimmon as Carly and I left for the bus.

Esma. Albert. Braveheart. Merciless. The words kept replaying themselves inside my head like a never-ending movie. As I entered the cafeteria with hordes of other students, the words seemed to be written everywhere. From the bathroom doors to the rubbery hot dog lying on someone's lunch tray.

I spotted an empty table near the back of the cafeteria, close to the exit which I mournfully observed. I couldn't wait until later that day when all students would be dismissed and sent back home. Just as I set my lunchbox down onto the table, I felt a slight tap on my shoulder.

"Mr. Rightpool?" I asked, expecting to see my sprightly gym teacher who had offered to play cards with me at lunch yesterday standing there, "If you want to play cards, I have to fetch them from my locker."

"There will be no need for that," a familiar voice said and I turned to find Sophia standing there. She was wearing a broad smile and a faint glimmer of mischief shone in the peculiar girl's eyes.

"Um, get away from me," I snapped, picking up my lunchbox in defense. I heard a few laughs come from my onlooking peers.

"My name's Sophia," said the girl, withdrawing her hand and smiling cordially. "But you already know that."

I dropped my lunch in fright, backing away from Sophia. Sophia had been one of the murderous girls in the cafeteria yesterday. The one who had killed Esma through some sort of Task Three.

"Esma," I cried, hitting the table with my legs as I backed away from the girl, "Esma. And yesterday, in the hallway. You seemed to be on bad terms with me."

"Oh, so you heard snippets of our talk," said Sophia, laughing and seeming to brush our previous skirmish aside, "That can all be explained in just a moment. Please do come and take a seat with my friends and me. Your name is Lexie, correct?"

"Yeah, you can call me that," I said, relaxing slightly, for Sophia seemed to be acting quite nice, "Only close friends and family call me Lex."

"Come along, Lexie," said Sophia, "And let's hope I get the honor of calling you Lex. Once you join the Black Sisterhood, of course."

I stared at the strange girl in confusion. The words pouring out of her mouth seemed unearthly and bizarre, but nonetheless, I followed her to a table by the floor to ceiling windows.

Everyone stared, wide-eyed and open-mouthed, suddenly looking at me with respect rather than sneers or smirks. I was puzzled. Was this her way of messing with me or did she truly want to befriend me?

We approached the table where Sophia sat with four other girls. One of them had long brown hair and wore a leather dress and fox-fur overcoat. She smiled coldly as I sat down next to Sophia. The other three girls seemed excited by my arrival. They all had blonde hair, blue eyes and wore jean jackets and leather pants.

"Well, this isn't some kind of circus act!" Sophia snapped at our onlooking peers and the noise level in the cafeteria steadily increased.

Sophia turned back to me with a smile playing on her lips, "Again, I'm Sophia. This is Cerise-" Sophia pointed at the girl wearing the leather dress- "Ah, and these are Bella, Ella, and Shella-" Sophia indicated the three blonde girls wearing jean jackets. They all simultaneously waved and I jumped a little.

"Are they triplets?" I asked fearfully, looking at the three girls.

Sophia laughed politely, "You'll get used to them, Lexie," she said, "They're not triplets, actually. Ever since they joined the Black Sisterhood, they've been stuck together like glue. Always dress the same, act the same, thankfully don't talk all at once, that would be a mess."

"Er, why did you invite me to sit with you?" I asked, trying not to look at Cerise who kept on shooting me nasty glares, "I mean, aren't I supposed to be the awkward new girl who no one likes?"

"Not to me, no," assured Sophia, "You seem interesting. You seem like someone who'd want to join The Black Sisterhood."

"Uh, what?" I asked, looking at Sophia with wide, puzzled eyes, "Er, is that like a study group or something?"

Cerise snickered and choked slightly on her water, exchanging a knowing look with Ella, Bella, and Shella. Sophia merely smiled and said:

"No, not quite. We're just a group of friends who's been working with the Mayor and police for years, stopping any crime from entering our town. It's not easy to get in our group though, Lexie."

"Huh?" I asked, getting angrier and more confused by the second, "Will you just fully explain everything to me?"

"I'm getting to that," said Sophia coolly, "You have to complete five tasks in order to join, but I will fully understand if you decide otherwise. Courage and wit is required for all of the tasks, especially the last one."

"Wha-what?" I asked, "But why me? You've only known me for one day? Isn't that too quick to assume?"

"You're unlike others," said Sophia, surveying me, "I allow everybody who wants to try out to try out, but rarely do I ever approach someone with the offer of trying out."

"Okay," I said, folding my trembling hands, "May I, um, see the tasks?"

"Certainly," said Sophia and pulled a crumpled paper out of her pocket, gently smoothing out the edges, "Here are the tasks. This paper has been through forty hands. Only five have made it in, including myself. Two have died."

Sophia passed me the paper and I looked over it:

Black Sisterhood

There are five tasks you must complete to join the Sisterhood. One task is to check your mind. One task is to check your eyes. One task is to check your heart. On one task you are helped by the leader, Sophia Persefoni. And the final task is the hardest of them all. See for yourself:

Task one: To check the mind, you are lined up in front of three simulations of dead bodies. You have five minutes per body to determine the cause of death of the person. You must accurately guess 3/3 to pass the test.

Task two: To check the eyes, you are to play a game of Russian Roulette with a jail prisoner. You are to complete four rounds without dying. It is up to your eyes and your mind to pass this test.

Task three: To check the heart, you will be put in a simulation where you will face your three greatest fears. You must stay there and fight them off for ten minutes. If you press the escape button before your ten minutes are up, you have failed.

Task four: Easiest of them all. With the help of Sophia, you will change your appearance to her liking. You must do whatever she says or you have failed.

Task five: Five simple but chilling words: Enter the House of Doom.

Get ready. You only get one chance. The Black Sisterhood doesn't accept failure.

I gulped and looked up at Sophia who tilted her head like a curious puppy, "Er, sorry to ask, but what is the House of Doom?"

Cerise choked on her sandwich, her eyes tearing up with mirth, "Never had someone this new here," she said.

"When the time comes, you'll see," said Sophia, ignoring Cerise, "You have to complete the other four tasks first. I mean, only if you're up to it."

"How exactly do you execute Task Three?" I asked nervously, "And isn't Task Two like illegal or something?"

"Advanced science is used for Task Three," said Ella, "Scientists all around West Virginia have helped us with Task Three since the beginning of The Black Sisterhood. And we have permission from the

Mayor for Task Two. We only take the prisoner that already looks dead to us, don't worry."

"Uh, but what if *I* die during one of these tasks?" I asked, nervously folding the corners of the paper.

Cerise laughed to herself as if it were the most hilarious thing in the world, "Then you don't join The Black Sisterhood."

"Then you die," said Sophia firmly, "Don't be afraid of death. It'll come sooner or later. It'll take us *all* at a point."

I felt sick to the stomach. Sophia had dragged me over to her table to give me a death wish. Too many things were happening at once.

"Before I decide upon joining The Black Sisterhood, may I ask, why are you so renowned? I mean, you're just a group of teenage girls, right?" I asked.

"My great great grandmother started this organization about a century ago," said Sophia, rather bitterly, "About four decades ago, my grandmother disgraced her family's legacy and quit The Black Sisterhood. My mother upstarted it once more and gained back the esteem from years before."

"Wow," I murmured, "Wow."

"So?"asked Bella, "We're all waiting to hear your final decision."

"Can I think about it?" I said, and Sophia took a deep breath, exhaling loudly.

"You have until the end of the day," she said, "Meet me after school at Locker 117. Bring nothing but your ultimate resolution."

A couple hours later, I was standing by Locker 117, my heart drumming loudly against my chest. Sophia hurried up to me, carrying a bag filled with darts. I shook off the thought of Sophia pelting me with those.

"What's that for?" I asked.

"Practice," said Sophia, "I practice my hand-eye coordination every now and then."

"Oh," I replied, leaning on the locker, "I've made up my mind."

"Alright," said Sophia, "I don't have all the time in the world."

"I'll try," I blurted out, not even thinking before. There was a burning desire within me, a desire to make new friends and take risks. "I'll try out."

"Good," said Sophia, smiling, "Talk later then." With that, she slung the bag over her shoulder and ran off towards the school courtyard.

I stood motionless by the locker, watching Sophia approach Cerise who was standing on the courtyard with more darts and a dartboard. Cerise glanced over at me and her menacing glance told me that my partake in The Black Sisterhood would be quite a rough ride in the beginning.

CHAPTER THREE

A month had passed since my talk with Sophia. I confronted her in the cafeteria every day, receiving vexed looks from Cerise. She brushed it off and told me the time would come when she talked to me herself. I had no choice but to nod along like an acquiescent pet.

Exactly a month later from my first talk with Sophia, I entered the kitchen to find Mom and Dad both sobbing. Mom sniveled into numerous boxes of tissues, pouring over a letter that lay in front of her.

I couldn't help but envision Mom locking lips with Albert as Dad kissed her on the cheek.

"Um, good morning?" I said, but received no response. Mom dug the heels of her hands into her eyes and continued wailing.

"Hi Lexie," said Mom, gasping for air after having cried, "Go ahead and pack yourself lunch."

"Uh, where's Carly?" I asked, cautiously approaching the two of them. Mom looked up at me as if I had just spat out a mouthful of curse words and began sobbing once more.

"That's just the thing," said Dad, sniffled slightly and wiped his eyes, "We woke up this morning and found a letter from Carly on the kitchen table. She said she was running away, God knows where. Why don't you take a look."

I took the folded note and opened it as Mom continued to cry and Dad joined in. My eyes watered as they skimmed over the letter which was written in hasty handwriting and soaked in tears from both Mom and Carly:

Mom, Dad, and Lexie, I swear I love you more than words can describe. You have given me everything over the past few years, but this is too much for me. I threw my phone into the lake a few miles from our house (very scenic, make sure to check it out), and ran away. I hate my new friends. They always gossip and are cruel to other students. I hate my classes and I hate this town. I'm going to try to run back to Pennsylvania and live with Nancy, my old friend. I love you, but I have to do this. I have to go.

Tons of questions flooded my mind, but I was too distressed to even bring any attention to them whatsoever. I keeled over and began to weep, bile rushing up my throat. Everything here in Parkersburg seemed to be unfolding in such a mysteriously uncanny way triggering me to scream loudly and slam the table in front of me.

"Lexie, you can stay home from school if you'd like," said Dad, rubbing Mom's arm.

"No," I said, feeling my temper rise, "I *want* to go to school, because school is the only place in this God-forsaken town where I can feel remotely safe!" With that, I crumpled up the note and threw it into the fireplace, where the raging fire swallowed the note while the logs smoldered, making crackling noises.

"Alexis, come back," said Dad angrily, "Copy down word for word what that note said, so we can hand it in to the police station."

"Not now," I snapped, slamming the door shut.

"Alexis, why are you going out so early? Your bus is due in half an hour," called Mom.

"I'm walking today," I snarled, "Just like I'm sick of everything else in this pathetic town, I'm sick of the bus. You haul Carly and me to a completely random state, and expect us to deal well with it, enjoy our new schools, and make friends when it's November and everyone already *has* friends. Little do you know, but I may die in a matter of time *because* of friends. Honestly, no wonder Carly ran away."

"Lex, what on earth are you talking about? Die because of friends? Do you hear yourself right now?" called Dad, staring at me as if I were a wild animal who must be tamed and controlled.

"Very clearly, thank you," I responded, not even turning around, "I should get going. The walk is pretty long." After having said that, I zipped up my coat tighter, and stuffed my hands into my pockets. The whole walk to school, I stared down at my feet blinded by rage, anxiety, guilt, tears, and so many other emotions.

I went through the morning at school like a zombie, occasionally snoozing in class and barely paying attention to what I was doing. Thanks to Sophia, people had stopped taunting me now but I still heard whispers pass between a few when I walked by.

As I made my way to an empty table in the cafeteria, someone pulled my hair playfully. I spun around and came face to face with Sophia.

"Oh, hey!" I half-yelled, half-whispered, and the cafeteria went silent to look at us.

"Get to it!" Sophia barked and everyone turned away, but I knew their ears were perked.

"Hey," I said, fiddling with the straps of my lunchbox, "Uh, did you want to talk about something?"

"Don' mind them," said Sophia, turning back to me, "All they want is something good to gossip about."

"Oh," I said, not quite sure who Sophia was talking about, "Do you mean the students?"

"Who else?" said Sophia, laughing coldly, "Anyways, we have to talk."

"You said the day would come when you approached me yourself," I said, grinning widely, "Am I doing the first task soon?"

Sophia's eyes glimmered again, "Yes, indeed," she muttered, as a few curious peers leaned towards us with conspicuously fake nonchalance.

"When? Today? Tomorrow?" I questioned, adrenaline rushing through my veins. I felt my heart pummel quickly against my ribs.

"Today," said Sophia, and leaned close to me to whisper something in my ear: "Do your parents know about you and The Black Sisterhood?"

"No, I haven't told them," I answered, "My sister ran away from home this morning. I take it they'll freak at the news if I tell them right now."

"Sorry to hear that," said Sophia, "Plan B, then. Come to 167 Camden Avenue at around midnight. It's Bella's house and I've got a few scientists to help do the dead body simulation. I have faith in you, Lexie."

Sophia walked back to her table and I remained standing, nonplussed. It pained me to think that I was using Carly's escape as an advantage to flee the house.

I floated in and out of sleep that night, my clammy hands grasping the corners of the nightstand. I woke up with a pounding heart and sweaty face, glancing nervously at the clock. Eleven struck and I slipped from my room, cautiously leaning over the banister.

Mom's skin was slick with a layer of sweat and she sobbed shakily. Dad was yelling at someone on the phone, looking incredibly frustrated.

"Sir, you're not giving me enough information," said the person on the other end, "If I receive any news on the location of Carly Torres, I will call you. Have a goodnight, sir."

A beeping sound rang through the otherwise silent air, indicating that the police officer had hung up. Mom shook with tears and Dad threw his phone to the ground. I took this as a chance to slope out the back door.

Culpability consumed me, though continuing seemed like a better option than turning back. The frigid early winter air struck me in the face, but I fought against the biting winds.

Bella's house was squat and short, designed in an archaic Victorian style manner. The shadows of five figures bounced off the walls of a room, and I entered the hushed house. Sophia, Bella, Ella, Shella, and two strangers greeted me. I felt a quiver run down my spine.

"Is Cerise not here?" I asked, and Sophia shook her head grimly.

"But you are!" cried Sophia, grabbing my hand and leading me over to a secluded room. Three beds stood in the room, a white blanket covering a hump in the center.

The two strangers turned out to be a man and a woman dressed in lab coats. The man wore a monocle and a very sour expression. The woman had pudding bowl hair and black glasses.

"My friends here from the lab have volunteered to help," said Sophia, gesturing at the man and woman behind her. They nodded curtly.

"I'm Roberto," said the man with a thick Spanish accent, "And this is my accomplice, Olga." The woman nodded, straightening her thick-framed glasses.

"They used mannequins and professionally designed them," said Ella, lips pursed, staring down at the humps with furrowed brows, "Very well done."

Bella walked into the room, flushed, "I locked the door and closed the windows," she said, "We're ready to get started."

"Great," said Sophia, flashing me a smile, "Five minutes per body. Good luck, Lexie."

She nodded at Olga and Roberto who removed the blanket off the first mannequin. My breath caught in my lungs. Fake arteries had been engraved along the mannequin's body. Its eyes were shut and its mouth hung loose. Forgery bloody marks could be seen on the mannequin's neck.

The clock ticked off time loudly behind me. I ran a finger along the mannequin's skin, shuddering at how unnaturally real it felt. The mannequin's neck was designed to look injured with a lengthy gash running along it.

Slit throat, I thought. Back in a self defense program I attended in seventh grade, we learned all about different terms and ways of murder. It was quite an unusual class, but proved useful. There seemed to be an unusual compression in the carotid arteries and jugular veins that had caused cerebral ischemia. The person had been strangled. Based on the neck, it had been-

"Ligature strangulation!" I cried, turning around so fast, I nearly slipped on the marble floor, "The mannequin was designed to be killed using ligature strangulation, meaning they were strangled with some kind of cord-like weapon like a garrote."

Sophia applauded lightly, "You sure know what you're doing," she said, "And you had quite a bit of time left. Roberto and Olga, if you'd please remove the cover off of the next mannequin."

This mannequin appeared to be bloated up. Its eyes bulged grotesquely and its tongue protruded out of its mouth. The mannequin's skin was malformed and slimy, bearing prodigious flaps of loose skin. Foam dribbled out of the mannequin's well-crafted lips.

The precision of the mannequin's design left me gawking at it for what seemed like hours. The way the skin of the mannequin was projected was astounding. Roberto and Olga ought to be highly esteemed experts.

"They drowned," I mumbled, my eyes glued to the mannequin, "Or someone drowned them."

Sophia hooted and pulled me into a hug, "Lexie, you're like a pro scientist," she said, "One more left."

I took a shaky breath, my feet automatically moving towards the last bed. Resisting the urge to cover my eyes, I watched as Olga removed the blanket. She looked exceptionally spiteful.

I had to cover my mouth with my hand to prevent a scream from spilling out. This mannequin looked quite unreal. A few hinges that connected the arms and legs were visible to me. It was covered in accurately drawn bruises and scratches. I noticed a huge, bloody crack in the mannequin's head.

The effect of blood clots being removed from the mannequin's brain had been put into place. The mannequin's leg was twisted in a horrific way. They appeared to have been viciously thrown off of something.

The clock ticked down the last seconds of doom and Olga said: "Ve will have to stop you soon. You have tventy seconds remaining."

Consternation hit me with full force, "A car crash?" I said, praying that it was correct. Olga let out a sharp, piercing laugh that made me shiver.

Ella, Bella, and Shella grinned and squealed like little kids. Roberto nodded brusquely and Olga stopped cackling mirthlessly when she realized I was correct.

The threesome pounced on top of me, howling mirthfully. I embraced all of them, grateful for their fortification. When Ella, Shella, and Bella cleared off,

I noticed Sophia standing regally in the center of the room.

"Task One, check," exclaimed Sophia and threw her arms around me, squeezing my rib cage. A sudden darkness filled me, gnawing at my innocence. The Black Sisterhood seemed to be sucking my chastity away. I welcomed it with graciousness.

CHAPTER FOUR

I threw myself into bed, limbs aching with exhaustion. I heard Mom crying into her pillow from across the hallway and guilt burned inside of my chest.

I saw the cloaked figure lingering by the house once more, but paid no attention to it. Dazed and groggy, I fell into an unperturbed sleep momentarily after my head hit the pillow.

Sophia had looked gleeful as she walked me home. She reminded me that I had four tasks left:

"Congratulations on completing Task One!" proclaimed Sophia, "Meet me tomorrow at seven in Black Tower Prison. Cerise and I are the only ones going. As you know, you have to play four rounds without dying. We've already selected the prisoner you'll be playing with. Anyways, see you around!"

"Bye!" I cried, receiving an amiable thump on the back from Sophia, "See you tomorrow!"

Time slipped through my fingers like sand. The driver waved goodbye to me as I left the bus, hurrying towards our new house. The mere thought of playing Russian Roulette with a criminal in Black Tower Prison frightened me.

"Where are you going, Lex?" asked Mom in a feeble voice as I attempted to slink out of the house.

"Project with friends," I answered roughly, "See you later." Barely acknowledging Mom's dubious stare, I hurried down the sidewalk. I stopped at Claire's for a drink before going to Black Tower Prison.

The bells in the door rang cheerfully as I entered. Only a couple people mulled around Claire's and I found an empty booth. A sprightly waitress skipped over to me and I ordered a milkshake.

The waitress left to the kitchen and I stretched, contemplating my chances of surviving Task Two. A spare copy of the town's newspaper from that morning caught my attention. I picked it up, smoothing out the crinkled edges and read the headline:

Keisha Allens and Tim Roberts
Go Missing in Parkersburg, West
Virginia

Last Seen with Olga Mikhailovna and
Roberto Fauci

I felt my blood freeze and my heart flutter. My eyes went down to the pictures of the missing people. My milkshake slipped out of my unpleasantly damp hands. It crashed to the floor, the glass shattering. The drowned man and the strangled woman. They had been real. That explained the great difference in the third mannequin, concerning the injuries.

Mortification infested my bones and I pushed past the waitress, tearing out of the shop. I had to get to Black Tower Prison and talk to Sophia about the dead people.

Cars honked at me from every angle, coming to screeching halts. I ran on, blinded by rage. The Black Sisterhood might've been in on this. Did they think they could get away with it?

Black Tower Prison looked a crematory from afar. It was an elongated building with a singular tall tower shooting up in the center. Black Tower Prison had musty, dark walls. Guards vigiled the entrances, holding guns. I stumbled up to one, still clutching the newspaper.

"Whad' you want?" drawled the guard, loading his gun, "Here to see anyone in particular?"

"I'm here for the Black Sisterhood," I said, glaring at the guard, "Sophia Persefoni called me."

The guard's eyes widened, "Ya here for the second task?" he asked.

"Yes," I said, "Move." The guard didn't resist and stepped to the side, letting me through. I jogged along a black corridor with spikes protruding from the walls. The lobby came into view and I pushed open the door, breathing in shallow pants.

The lobby was a stocky room with dingy walls. Dead stink bugs were stuck in the overhead lights. Plastic chairs stood around the room, facing outward. The door swung open and a police officer stepped in, holding a man in handcuffs.

The police officer came up to the front desk, "Get him detained for the time being. Caught in the act of robbing a bank," he said. The delinquent scowled at me, narrowing his eyebrows. I quickly looked away.

"Oh, you're here early," said a familiar voice behind me, "The prisoner is ready."

Sophia and Cerise stood a little ways away from me, holding a Russian Roulette game. Sophia smiled and threw me the game. I let it fall to the ground and brandished the newspaper in her face.

"Lexie, what's going on?" asked Sophia, picking up the game. Cerise drew back with a disparaging smile crossing her countenance.

"Look!" I shrieked, attracting stares from all around the room. Sophia pressed her index finger against my lips and I stomped my foot on the ground, pushing her away.

Sophia snatched the newspaper out of my hands, nearly tearing it apart. Her eyes enlarged with terror as she read the headline and looked at the picture: "Lexie, I swear, I d-d-didn't know they used real humans for t-t-two of the things," she stuttered.

"Quit the fake act," I snarled, "They've been your accomplices for a long time. I don't see why they would do this, out of the blue."

"Alexis, stop!" exclaimed Sophia, her voice going up a notch, "Roberto and Olga aren't my accomplices. Alice and Charlie are my accomplices.

They're husband and wife. Alice and Charlie went on a vacation together, not knowing a newcomer was soon doing Task One."

Sophia dropped the newspaper and cried, wiping her eyes with the sleeve of her shirt. I slapped my arm on my leg, getting more confused by the second.

Cerise rubbed Sophia's arm consolingly. Her usual sneer had been wiped clean off her face.

"Let's go confront Roberto and Olga," Cerise said determinedly, "Do you know where they could be?"

Sophia nodded, continuously wiping her eyes: "They work at the Institution of Forensic Pathology. Once my accomplices' vacation came to my knowledge, I began rifling through so many documents, trying to find two decent people. That's why it took so long to prepare Task One, Lexie," she said, blinking back tears, "I'm awfully sorry."

I mustered up a smile, "I forgive you, Sophia," I said, "They seemed like aloof people, but I didn't know it was possible to be that heartless."

Sophia looked slightly more valiant as she said: "Cerise is right. We have to get Roberto and Olga locked up. Let's go. Sophia walked up to the lady at the front desk and told her that Task Two was postponed.

The winds hit my face sharply, but I kept running. Fury and adrenaline pumped through my body. It almost seemed as if some kind of invisible force was pushing me along, no energy drained.

Sophia, Cerise, and I burst through the doors of the Institution of Forensic Pathology . We hurried through the front lobby. The security guards yelled for us to stop but we kept running.

"Where are those scumbags?" muttered Cerise, sweat forming on her forehead. Cerise was finally showing her true colors, meaning she could be a good person if she wanted to.

A screech protruded from Sophia's throat, bringing me back to actuality. I followed her malevolent stare to Roberto and Olga. They and a few other scientists were leaning over a body, exchanging trivial talk.

"Performing an autopsy?" I asked, giving them a condescending glare, "Did you kill this person, too? Or did they die of their own cause?"

Roberto dropped a tool with a resounding *clang!*

and Olga gaped at me. The other scientists stopped to stare, forgetting about the dead body in front of them.

"Vut are you talking about, Miss Alecksis?" questioned Olga, recovering from her momentary state of shock, "Get out of our laboratory before ve call ze police on you girls!"

"Show her the newspaper," whispered Cerise into my ear. Olga plucked the newspaper out of my hands. She scanned the headline, her eyes dropping to the picture. Olga thrust the newspaper into Roberto's hands. He whimpered and threw himself to the ground, sobbing.

Olga glared at him disdainfully, ripping the newspaper into pieces and chucking it into the recycling bin:

"Vut is your evidence now, girls?" she asked, smirking.

"Sorry to break it to you, but that' not the only newspaper in town," I said, "The police station isn't far from here and you two are coming with us."

Sophia and Cerise lunged onto Roberto and Olga and pinned them to the ground. Cerise slammed her fist in Olga's face. Olga cowered back, blood spewing out of her nose. Sophia yanked Roberto up with a fiendish pull of his hair. Cerise grabbed Olga, squeezing her hands together.

The other scientists shrieked in terror, backing away from Roberto and Olga. The guards seized the two killers, dubiously staring at the body.

"Stay here," said one of the guards, "We'll take them to the police station."

"Wait!" cried Sophia," We want to hear them out. Hear their explanation as to why they did that and betrayed The Black Sisterhood."

"It's not only about the stupid Black Sisterhood!" yelled Cerise, "Two innocent people were slaughtered! Sophia, will you please open your eyes?!"

"Everyone, cut it out!" I screamed, standing up on a chair, "Calm down!"

"What do you want us to do, Sophia?" asked the other guard.

"Go to the police station," I interrupted, "We'll stay behind. Tell the police to record everything and have it automatically download to a flash drive. Bring the flash drive back."

"Okay," grunted the guard, heaving Olga up, "We'll bring your flash drive."

They began towing Roberto and Olga behind them. Everyone in the Institution of Forensic Pathology were still screaming, clutching on to one another. Roberto and Olga screamed haunted screams of a killer. A killer awaiting its death. I shivered and turned back, feeling that something was wrong.

Cerise and Sophia hugged, crying into each other's shoulders. Time slipped by. I sat against a wall, head buried in my legs. The cool of the wall pulsed into my head, a brisk refreshment. It pained me to think that this was my fault. If I had never come along, Alex and Claire would be on vacation and Sophia wouldn't have to hire Roberto and Olga. Keeping my head down would've been so much better.

"No, it wouldn't," a soft voice said behind me. I looked up to find Cerise. Her eyes looked assuaging and relaxed me when I looked into them. No smirks, no nothing. Just a smile.

"Cerise? What do you mean by that?" I asked, drawing back. Sophia was still sitting on the floor.

Cerise pressed her hand against the wall, leaning in. She smelled of pine trees and cumin. The smell was irresistible.

"I can't read minds, but I can read your eyes," continued Cerise, "You're thinking along the lines of keeping your head down. But trust me, there's something coming. You'll be a tremendous help if you keep your head up. A moment of history will be revealed within a month. A moment none of us want to relive."

Her chilling words rung in the air. Cerise pushed herself away and went to join Sophia, who was huddled in a corner. A couple minutes passed, a knot of tautness forming in my chest.

The guards finally came back with frightened countenances. One of them handed us a green flash drive. Cerise immediately sprung to her feet and Sophia woke up.

"Got about ten death threats from those two ~til the police came," he said gruffly, "Tol' them police ~bout you girls. Know the Black Sisterhood, them police. Got the flash drive."

"Thanks," I said, "Sophia, can you please go find a computer?"

Sophia nodded and hurried off. She glanced over her shoulder before disappearing behind a door.

Cerise came up to me with a smile: "Hey, I heard about how well you completed the first task," she said. I threw her a fervent look and rolled my eyes, turning to face the other way. The first task. With the murdered people. Yep, I did great.

"Sorry, I suppose that's a weak topic for you right now?" she asked, and I suppressed a grin. Just a few hours ago, Cerise was throwing me cold looks and smiles. Now she was acting perfectly friendly.

"Yeah," I grunted, and spun around. Cerise looked hopeful that I would make small talk with her. I looked right past her at Sophia who was running towards us with a computer.

"I got the computer, guys," she said, wheezing, "Had to run-" she stopped and waved her hand in circles with short breaths, "Heck of a way."

Sophia led us over to a table close by and placed the computer down:

"Let's take a look," said Cerise, and we all huddled around the computer. I fingered the flash drive nervously and then plugged it in, taking a deep breath. The truth was about to be revealed.

The video came to action. It was a small, worn down room with blank walls. An air vent howled loudly in the corner and the air conditioner hummed. A police officer sat in a pouffy white chair, while Roberto and Olga both sat in hard wooden chairs without a back to lean on. Their hands were in cuffs behind the chair, in an uncomfortable looking position.

"Why did you murder Keisha Allens and Tim Roberts?" the police officer asked, fiddling with his badge, "What was your initiative or objective?"

"It vas for ze Black Sisterhood," said Olga, her face a nasty shade of green. Roberto's tongue lolled out of his mouth and he sagged off the chair.

"Say that again?" the officer said.

"Ze Black Sisterhood!" roared Olga, spit flying from her mouth, "Sophia Persefoni's ancestors created zis monster-hood."

"Oh,"the officer said and his face went blank, "I know exactly what you're talking about. Go ahead."

"It vasn't ve who killed ze Keisha Allens and Tim Roberts," continued Olga, "Vell, it vas us, but ve vere forced by a specific someone to do it."

"And who is that specific someone?" asked the officer, "Is she a member of the Black Sisterhood?"

"No, sir. Ve have known zis man for only two veeks," said Olga, "He confronted us not long after Sophia gave us a call, asking if ve could replace her accomplices, Alex and Charlie for ze Black Sisterhood."

"And?" the officer asked, raising his eyebrow in mock disbelief.

"He told us to kill ze people for two of the things, and use a mannequin for one," Olga continued, but it looked as if she was having difficulty speaking. Her face was turning purple and veins in her temple were throbbing.

"Ok, we can discuss all that later,"the officer said, waving it off, "Who is this man?"

"Alvays vears a cloak, but he revealed his face, mister," said Olga, "Zis person is- AAAH!"

Olga suddenly clutched her neck. She groaned and collapsed onto the floor, thrashing around before going still. Roberto's eyes widened. Not long after, he also grabbed his neck and met the same fate as Olga.

"TURN OFF THE DAMN CAMERA!" the officer yelled. The camera was muffled and moans came from somewhere beyond. The last thing we saw was the officer removing chips from Roberto's and Olga's necks.

"Guys, what were those chips in Roberto and Olga's necks?" I asked. The guard standing by us nodded acerbically.

"Yeah, what were they?" asked Sophia and we all turned to face the guard who looked as insipid as us. He shrugged mournfully:

"All the police officer found was them chips. Reckons someone placed those chips into their necks. And they ain't tracking chips, they be special killing chips," said the guard in a light tone, "You girls stay out of trouble now, okay?"

"Yeah," I lied, sweat beading at my forehead, "We'll stay out of trouble."

Pictures of Roberto and Olga being brutally murdered resurfaced. I crumpled to the floor, Sophia and Cerise grabbing my arms.

"Go back home," the guard said, waving us off, "Y'all have already been in enough trouble today."

"Let's go," said Sophia as she handed the flash drive back to the guard. We walked along the halls in silence, the scientists recoiling away from us.

Roberto and Olga had been so close to revealing who forced them. Then they died, clutching their necks. Something didn't add up.

Snow came down in torrents outside, slashing across the windows of people's homes. Cerise branched off from us, walking down a different road. I saw her huddle down by a trash can near a lovely home.

"Cerise!" a sharp voice said, "Get in!" A woman holding a mop had come out. She grabbed Cerise by the collar and forced her inside the house. I looked away, tears burning at my eyes.

Sophia looked deathly cold. She pressed herself against my chest, absorbing my body heat. Her thin legs trembled and a gust of wind swept through the alley, toying with her hair. Something broke in me: Roberto and Olga dying, Cerise being hit by the mop…"

"I have to stop," said Sophia, "I'm terribly cold. I-I-I am going to get a cup of tea at Claire's. Lexie, Task Two has been cancelled for you. Your bravery outshone everything. See you tomorrow in school."

Claire's sign flashed in bright letters above my head. Sophia hustled into the cafe, waving one last time. I smiled broadly. Not only was my life spared, but the life of the prisoner was too. And even though he was a crook, he still had a right to live and not die because of a foolish game.

I smiled feebly in hopes to raise my mood, but no happiness came.

When I came home, shivering with cold, I found Mom sitting on the steps and crying.

"Uh, Mom, are you okay?" I asked. Mom bustled over to me and swept me into a hug. She cried, snot dribbled down her face.

"I thought you were dead, Lex!" screeched Mom, nearly snapping my neck in half, "With Carly missing and all, God knows what could've happened to you out there!"

"It's okay, Mom, I'm fine," I mumbled, "And, uh, I think it's best if I tell you something that has been going on."

I was about to disclose to Mom about the Black Sisterhood. Guilt surged through me every time I snuck out of the house.

"Yes?" said Mom, "You can discuss anything with me, dear. Let's just go inside first."

Mom pushed open the door, steering me in by the shoulders. It creaked miserably filling me with an odd despair.

"Where's Dad?" I asked, looking around at the dark, empty house. Mom sighed and answered:

"Your father hasn't been the same, I'm afraid. He got a call from work an hour ago and had to go. Strangely distant from me, you, and the situation with Carly. He has made plenty of money for us, though."

"Yeah," I said, hanging up my coat. Mom knelt down beside me and ran her hand up and down my leg.

"So what's been bothering you?" she asked, "Is everything alright?"

"Er, well, I just, um, thought I'd tell you that the project with my friends is going great," I said, getting cold feet at the last moment.

"I knew you'd accustom to Parkersburg soon enough," said Mom delightedly, "Get some sleep now."

I waddled up to my room, feeling disconcerted and numb. I heard the indistinct sound of a door opening and closing downstairs. Maybe Dad was home.

Olga had said the killer wore a cloak. I hesitantly peered out the window. He was still there. Silent, eerie, cloaked. I grabbed the curtains to steady myself, breathing through my mouth.

Could it be the one I saw every night? Could he be dangerous? Could he have put the chips in Olga's and Roberto's necks? And as the figure slipped away into the woods beyond the abandoned house, two more distressing thoughts occurred to me: Was the Black Sisterhood in danger? Was I?

CHAPTER FIVE

Ava, Midge, and a few other of my newly acquired friends laughed and joked along with me as we ate lunch. I still shuddered at last night's events, but managed to forget about it. Sophia approached me, grinning. Ava choked on her sandwich and quickly looked away. Midge snorted and stared at Ava with a pitiful stare I couldn't quite discern.

"Hey, Lexie," she said and I stood up to talk to her, "I just have to tell you something."

"In private?" I asked but Sophia shook her head. She seemed to welcome the fact that everyone had once again stopped to listen to our conversation.

"Every year I have a small movie night," began Sophia, "I usually don't have time for things like that, but that movie night has been a tradition of The Black Sisterhood for decades. I always take my boyfriend and two other friends. They don't necessarily have to be in the Black Sisterhood, like when I took Tony and Christie last year. Christie was too chicken to try out and Tony failed Task One."

"Oh, okay," I said, not exactly sure how to respond to this, "So, who're you taking this year?"

Sophia cracked a smile: "That's just the point," she continued, "This year, I'm taking Cerise and you. Cerise has never gone to movie night with me which I know has saddened her, and you, my friend, are very close to becoming part of the Sisterhood. But that's not the only reason why. You're my close friend, Lexie, that's why. It makes me happy to be around you."

This made me shine with joy. Everyone broke out into whispers and the girls I was sitting with eyed me with envy. I looked around at the Black Sisterhood table and saw Bella, Ella, Shella, and Cerise all waving at me with smiles.

"Thanks, Sophia," I rambled, "That means a lot. Who's your boyfriend? When's the movie night? Sorry, am I asking too many questions?"

Sophia laughed and jokingly punched me in the shoulder: "You sound like a kid going to the toy store," she chuckled, "Meet me tonight at The Orion Theatre at eight o'clock. My boyfriend's name is Dillon. You'll see him tonight, his father is dropping him off because his motorcycle got a flat tire."

"Can I meet him now?" I asked, and Sophia shook her head, a mysterious glint in her eyes:

"Surprises are meant to be surprises," she said, "See you tonight at eight. We'll discuss Task Three after the movie."

"Hey, tell Ella that Ava says hi," cried Midge, and Sophia's face darkened slightly. I didn't give the comment much thought, for Sophia's invitation was my top priority at the moment.

"Bye!" I cried enthusiastically as Sophia walked off. Tonight was going to be great. And I didn't even have to lie to Mom and Dad about where I was going.

The girls around me were chirping with animation, waving their hands and asking me how it felt to be friends with Sophia.

I responded with a mischievous smile Sophia would've been proud of: "Feels great to be friends with Sophia," I said, "But it'll feel even better to be sisters."

Midge, who I detested most out of everyone else, raised her eyebrow indignantly and asked: "Um, please elaborate. What do you mean sisters?"

"Oh, but isn't it obvious, Midge" Ava asked in a condescending way, "Part of the Black Sisterhood. Everyone in the Black Sisterhood share blood."

"Share blood?" I asked, "Literally?"

"Yes," said Ava seriously, "I know it isn't listed as one of the tasks, but once you complete all the tasks you share blood by cutting your hand just a bit."

"How d'you know all this?" I asked.

"Hmph," said Ava, and this appeared to be a weak topic for her, "Ella and I used to be best friends. We were inseparable. Never saw one of us without the other. That was until, of course, she caught whiff of the fact that the Black Sisterhood existed. At first she told me about everything. Ella was the latest member to join. She told me about Bella, Shella, Cerise and Sophia. She told me about all the tasks and we were still best friends forever until after Task Four."

"What happened?" asked Midge, and I threw her a look of disgust. I could tell she knew, but just wanted to push Ava for bad memories to resurface.

Ava sighed and closed her eyes, "I still reduce to tears to this day whenever I remember how close the two of us used to be," she said, and a tear flew from her squeezed shut eyes. I saw Midge scoff disapprovingly into her lunch.

"Did she get too close to Sophia?" I asked, sympathizing with Ava. I knew how she felt. I once had a friend like that in third grade. Of course she didn't leave me for a gang, she just left me for a different group of girls.

"Yeah," said Ava, "Came to school the next morning with her hair dyed blonde. She was wearing leather pants and had piercings in a few areas. She looked stunning, but I knew we'd never be good friends again from that moment on. She started kinda ignoring me after that, occasionally talking to me, and then after Task Five-poof! Not a single word. Was now part of that disgusting filthy squad."

"So how'd you know about sharing the blood?" I questioned, and the other girls who hadn't heard this part of the story yet, leaned in closer to Ava to hear her better.

"Saw her scar," replied Ava, "I asked her if she was okay and she just mumbled about sharing the blood with that clan of hers. Felt like slapping the hell out of her. How dare she join that slimy, grimy, disgusting gang and not tell me a word. That Sophia Persefoni is the devil in disguise, dunno why everyone's so obsessed with her. I can almost see the red horns poking out of her greasy hair. And don't even get me started on that idiot, Cerise. She should just grab a big ol' shovel, dig up a nice hole for her big head, crawl in there, and rot-"

BAM! That was all it took for me to hit Ava in the face with all my might. Her face went back as if attached to her neck with springs and blood leaked from her mouth. She glared at me, and Midge put her hand under the table to give me a high-five. I didn't care about how much I hated Midge right now. I returned the high-five underneath the table and focused back onto Ava who was bleeding like crazy.

The girls around her didn't know what to do. They probably thought that siding with me would bring them closer to the Black Sisterhood, but siding with Ava would keep them out of trouble and save their friendship with her.

A few of the girls came to stand with Midge and me, while the others hurried to get a teacher.

People crowded around us, whispering something in alarmed tones.

I felt a nudge and saw Sophia flanked by her friends standing next to me. Her face was contorted into many different emotions: pride, perplexion, worry, and more.

"Lexie, what was that all about?" asked Shella, staring at me in awe.

"Follow me to the bathroom," I grumbled and we sneaked off to the ladies' restroom. We shut ourselves in a stall and I began to explain:

"Ava was saying how she and Ella used to be really good friends until Ella joined the Black Sisterhood. Said Ella would tell her everything until Task Four when she bonded with Sophia. And after Task Five, Ava said there was no getting her back."

"And that's why you whammed her in the face with all your might?" asked Sophia with pursed lips.

"No!" I cried frustratedly, "Ava started insulting the Black Sisterhood. She called you, Sophia, the devil. She called the Black Sisterhood a grimy and disgusting gang, and told Cerise to dig a large hole for her big head, crawl in there, and die."

Cerise's face resembled nothing but fury. Sophia bent her head down and grinned:

"Omigosh, Lexie, I'm impressed," she said, "Standing up for the Black Sisterhood is one rule you must follow. Congrats, girl, that just made you more deserving of going with Cerise and me tonight to the movies."

For a split second, I saw Cerise's face contort with bliss, but it quickly went back to utter rage. Although her sudden warmth towards me was bizarre, I was glad to accustom so quickly to The Black Sisterhood.

We suddenly heard someone enter the bathroom and quickly stepped onto the toilet so no one would see our feet. My euphoria of being complimented so graciously by Sophia rapidly turned into fear burning inside my veins.

"Lexie better come out if she's in here," a deep voice which I recognized as the principal's boomed, "She should know we aren't going to get her into trouble."

"Go out," Bella hissed in my ear, and gently pushed me off the toilet. I unlocked the stall door with a deep breath and pushed it open, slamming it behind me so as not to reveal the other girls.

"Ah, Alexis Torres," said the principal, smiling meekly. He was surrounded by the school's vice principal and Ava herself. I felt it quite unethical that Mr. Borren had so boldly strode into the ladies' restroom.

"M-m-mr. Borren, what are you doing in the girls' bathroom?" I asked nervously as Ava smirked. I froze when I realized that the principal saying I wasn't going to get in trouble was a way to coax me out. I heard a light gasp in the stall where the Black Sisterhood was. They had realized that too.

"Come to get you, Miss Torres," replied the principal.

"S-s-shall I follow you to your office?" I questioned, shaking from head to toe as I realized Principal Borren was probably going to call Mom and Dad.

"No need," Principal Borren said consolingly, and Ava dropped her smile, "We'll make it simple and clear. Physically assaulting another student is, of course, unacceptable, but you did it for the good of the Black Sisterhood. Sophia has informed us of your excellence during Task One, and how you caught two murderers red-handed. Well, forced murderers. The chips are still being investigated. We will let you off the hook with a clean record this one time, but never again, Lexie, never again."

With that, Principal Borren smiled again and walked out of the bathroom followed by the vice principal. Ava threw me one last nasty look before stalking out.

Sophia, Cerise, Bella, Ella, and Shella walked out of the stall they were in, stunned.

"Well, you're good to go," said Sophia, smiling, "Can't believe that just happened, but I guess Principal Borren's right."

"Yeah," I mumbled, looking down at the floor, "Um, I think we should probably go back to class. This has been an interesting lunch, but I'll see you guys later."

It wasn't fair for me to get off the hook like that. I was glad I had, but Ava was hurt mentally and physically. Mentally, I could understand how hurt she had been when Ella had left her. It wasn't Ella's fault, or Sophia's fault, or Ava's fault, it was just the way the world worked.

I felt guilty and horrible for my deed, and needed to apologize to Ava as soon as possible. Just because I was most likely going to get into the Black Sisterhood didn't mean I wanted to have a reputation for being a temperamental person. I knew Sophia, Cerise, Bella, Ella, and Shella were confused by my sudden escape from the bathroom, but I could explain everything to them later.

"Woah, there!" someone cried from behind me, "Keep those fists in your pockets!"

I raised my fist up and the trio of boys ran away, giggling like toddlers.

Back to Square One, I thought, violently jerking my locker door open.

"I'm going to the movies with my friends, Mom, see you later!" I yelled, a couple hours since school's release.

"Okay, honey, I'll see you later!" Mom yelled back, and I opened my phone to google the directions to The Orion Theatre. It was a little ways from here, and I set off, chilly wind flying around my bare ankles.

When I arrived at The Orion Theatre, my face was stinging with cold and flushed a light pink color.

I saw Sophia, Cerise, and a boy my age standing with his father in the front lobby, apparently waiting for me.

"Hey, guys!" I cried, waving. Sophia turned around, beamed, and embraced me tightly. Cerise just smiled and waved.

"Hey, guys," I whispered, and Cerise and Sophia clustered around me, "Uh, sorry about today in the bathroom during lunch. I just felt really bad for what I had done and didn't really know what to do-"

"It's fine, we understand," said Cerise, smiling amiably, "I would've felt the same way, but honestly, you did nothing wrong. We all make mistakes, and that was just a weak moment, even though you meant well."

I bent my head down. Cerise comforting me was the last thing I had expected. I could tell we all knew that, because the tension was so great one could break it with a knife.

Sophia clapped her hands, breaking the strain: "Yeah, you're fine, Lexie. We get it, it's okay. Er, Dillon, my boyfriend, is waiting for us, his Dad already left. Let's go."

We all nodded and Sophia beckoned Dillon to come over to us. I felt a hot flush rising up my cheeks. Although I didn't exactly find Dillon attractive, there was something within me that felt envious of Sophia. With his slick blonde hair, large blue eyes, and chiseled cheekbones, he looked like a movie star. Sophia gave him a small kiss on the cheek and turned back to us.

"Er, what movie are we watching?" I asked.

"A new version of Les Miserables came out, and I'm super excited to see it!" cried Sophia, grabbing Dillon's arm and leading us to the movie theatre, "I already paid for the tickets for all of us and the movie starts in five minutes. Let's get going!"

I dozed off a couple times during the movie which was a little boring, but it was nice to spend time with Sophia, Cerise, and Dillon. I did have to admit; it was bothersome to turn around and find Sophia and Dillon constantly locking lips.

After the movie, we all stood up and stretched, our limbs cracking like firecrackers. Sophia gave me a meaningful look and turned to Dillon: "I have to go to the bathroom, D," she said, looking at Dillon with wistful eyes, "I'll be right back."

"Er, can Lexie and I come with you, Sophia?" asked Cerise, and she nodded. We all hurried off to the restroom, leaving Dillon behind.

The restroom was flooding with women, girls, teenagers, and a couple toddlers which was good news for us. It would block out our speech so no one could hear.

"Wait, Sophia, does Dillon not know about the Black Sisterhood?" I asked.

"Not surprised you asked," replied Sophia with a wink in my direction, "I know I've been acting as if he doesn't know, but of course he does. I've been telling him that you're just a friend of mine, because I want it to be a surprise for him when you get in."

"It's not guaranteed I will, though," I said, and Sophia shook her head, chuckling.

"Even if you don't, we'll all still be great friends," said Sophia and Cerise nodded her consensus.

"But won't he find out sooner or later?" I asked, "I mean, everyone else already knows, right? So with the rumors going around, I reckon he'll find out. Give it a few days or so."

"Been trying to steer him away from all of that," responded Sophia, giggling. She was blushing slightly and I felt a pain of covetousness, sincerely hoping it didn't show on my face. I could see Cerise fighting a deep feeling inside of her, too. We both exchanged glances that spoke a million words and quickly turned back. We didn't want Sophia to notice, for she'd be far too upset.

"Er, guys, is everything okay?" Sophia asked, and I felt a blush creeping up the side of my cheeks.

"Yeah, we're just tired," said Cerise hastily, "Can we discuss Task Three and go home already?"

"Aight, if you two are so tired at like ten p.m., then let's get talking," said Sophia, sniggering, "Lexie, we don't want the whole Black Sisterhood coming to Task Three. There's going to be plenty of scientists already, trust me. It's a complicated process, but you'll manage."

"Okay," I said, "So, who's coming then?"

"I mean, I'm obviously coming since I am Head of the Black Sisterhood, and you can choose one more person to come," said Sophia regally, "The choice is all yours. So, Cerise, Bella, Ella, or Shella?"

"Cerise," I said automatically, and Cerise's smile was so large it could've taken up a whole football field, "I want Cerise to come."

"Great!" cried Sophia, "So, Cerise be there tomorrow at nine p.m., okay? Lexie, does that work for you?"

"Yeah, but where is there?" I asked, slightly puzzled.

"The location changes for every person, depending on their greatest fears. I need you to tell me your three greatest fears. We'll go from there," said Sophia.

"Er," I said, completely blanking, "Definitely spiders is one of them, I can't stand those creepy, hairy things." I stopped, and a smirk spread inside me. I knew this would be considered cheating, but I could come up with three fake fears so that Task Three would be a piece of cake.

"Um, Lexie, sorry if it's not my place to say this, but we'll know by your body language in the simulation if you lied to us," said Cerise. She could "read" my mind. Damn it.

"Oh, okay," I said coolly, "Great, so, er, spiders is one. Another is my family and friends in danger.

And my final one-" I paused. What was another fear of mine?

"Take your time and state your biggest fears," whispered Sophia and I nodded.

"Heights," I said, shivering at the thought, "I'm absolutely petrified of them."

"Splendid," said Sophia, smiling vaguely and clapping her hands, "Can you give me your phone number, Lexie?"

"Yeah," I said, and Sophia handed me a small sticky note and pen from her purse. I wrote my phone number on it and handed it back to her. She scanned it and typed the number into her contacts.

"I will discuss with the scientists and text you as soon as I get the chance. You'll have your answer by nine p.m. tomorrow, without a doubt. Now I suggest we get going, D must be getting worried," said Sophia.

Again. That feeling of spite suffocated me, and I fought to keep my face from contorting into resentment. I looked at my feet, and shuffled out the door, followed closely by Cerise whose head was also bent.

"Dillon just texted me. He's already outside with his father," said Sophia. Cerise and I followed Sophia out of The Orion Theatre, heads still down.

Dillon was waiting with a tall, skinny man who was proudly patting a sleek red Ferrari. Sophia swept over to Dillon, kissed him, and turned back to us with a large grin plastered on her face.

"D, tell your Dad to greet our guests," said Sophia, and Dillon muttered something in his father's ear. His father who was just as alluring as him turned around, smiling broadly.

My mouth went dry. Was it who I thought it was?

"Hey kids, my name's Albert," said Dillon's dad, and I felt like keeling over and vomiting. It was the man I had seen Mom cheating on Dad with. My heart skipped a few beats at once and I felt faint.

Albert caught my eye and quickly looked away, dropping his hat: "Hi, you're the new girl, Alexis Torres, right? Yeah, I saw your Mom at Claire's a couple weeks ago," he prated, sweating slightly.

Dillon threw me a look of confusion, and I shrugged. The only person who I wanted to talk to about this was Cerise. I couldn't trust Sophia because she would go babbling to Dillon. Bella, Ella, and Shella seemed like nice enough people, but I just didn't know them all too well.

"Er, well, bye," said Dillon, and hastily climbed into his car.

Cute, but awfully rude, I thought with crossed arms and a disdainful sneer. Sophia waved goodbye, told us she was going with Dillon, climbed into the car and they drove off.

I turned to Cerise: "Um, I have to tell you about something, Cerise," I mumbled, "That man, Dillon's father, has had a few affairs with my Mom. I found out about that like two days after we moved to Parkersburg, but he doesn't know I know, and neither does my Mom. I don't know what to do."

"Oh my God," said Cerise, "Really?" I nodded with watering eyes.

I was about to say something when I noticed a cloaked figure standing a few feet away from me. Its head was bent, and covered with the black cloak that shrouded the rest of its body.

"Cerise, I have to go," I said, turned around, and ran away. That cloaked figure seemed to be everywhere I went. Next to my house, right here by the movie theatre... It was quite haunting, and I couldn't help but wonder: Who was that and what did they want from me?

CHAPTER SIX

It was one o'clock in the morning when my phone buzzed. It was a text from Sophia. The text read: *Hey, just talked to the scientists can you come tomorrow to the testing bureau of verified virology?*

My brain felt like it had been stuffed with cotton balls but I awoke on the inside when I read the text. The location had been determined for Task Three, and I quivered with both anxiety and excitement. I rubbed my eyes and wrote back to Sophia:

Of course, I'll be there tomorrow at nine p.m., not a minute late not a minute early.

A read receipt and typing awareness indicator both popped up. Sophia was replying: *Atta girl! Task 3 is always in some kind of science lab because they need a lot of space for it. Yours needs more space than most, to be quite frank.*

OK, I'll see you tomorrow at school. So sorry, but I need to sleep since I wake up early for the bus.

I was still zonked and worn-out, even though Sophia's first text had perked me up a bit. The typing indicator popped up once more and figuring Sophia was just going to bid me good night, I placed my phone back on the counter.

I slowly started drifting back to sleep when my phone began to ring maniacally. I picked it up, irritated and sour, when I realized it was still Sophia, spamming the M out of Monday:

No, Lexie you can't go to school tomorrow! I say this to everyone before task three!! You need to fake being sick & then sneak out at night! Do your parents go to bed early?

I was perplexed. Sophia wanted me to skip school, feign being sick, and then sneak out at night to a completely unfamiliar laboratory? I rolled my eyes. If it was for the greater good, I would probably do what she said. Fatigued and rancorous, I began to type back:

You want me to pretend being sick & then sneak off at night??? Sure, I can do that, my parents have been going crazy about finding Carly. Mostly my mother, my father is constantly inundated with work. Seems a bit unrealistic, don't you think?

Well if he works night shifts, follow him to work one night on your mom's car. You know how to drive, right?

Er, slightly, I suppose it doesn't require much skill to follow someone who's in clear sight. If I luck out, I can get back tonight just in time.

Great, well you should sleep anyways for the upcoming task. It's going to be a rather convoluted endeavor, but I have faith in you.

Okay, I will see you tonight.

See you!

The prospect of skipping school that day was exciting, but guilt pressed on my conscience when I realized I would be sneaking out again and not telling Mom and Dad. If I lucked out, I'd have enough time to follow Dad to work and see what he had really been up to.

I laid my phone back on my cabinet, thinking how I would feign being sick. An ingenious idea popped up in my brain and I tiptoed downstairs to the bathroom. We kept the thermometer and other medicines in the top cabinet. I clambered up, trying not to make too much noise, got the thermometer, and went to the kitchen where I made myself a steaming cup of tea.

I sidled back upstairs, placed the cup of tea on my cabinet, and dipped the thermometer into the hot tea. It sizzled for a second, and when I took the thermometer out, the temperature was 39 Celsius. There was no way Mom could let me off with that temperature.

I fake-sneezed loudly, and sighed as if struggling. I heard soft footsteps coming up the stairs and Mom opened the door. I put on the sickest look I could manage and handed Mom the thermometer.

"I think I have a fever and cold," I croaked, massaging my throat as if it pained.

Mom's eyes widened: "Stay home today, Lexie," said Mom, "I'll bring you some medication and I see you've already made yourself tea."

"Yeah," I mumbled, culpability still stabbing at my soul, "You and Dad still looking for Carly?"

Mom's eyes narrowed significantly: "I'm starting to get suspicious with your father and where he's really going. He has a night shift today at eleven p.m., whad' you think about following him?" questioned Mom.

"Er, yeah, I'll definitely get better by that time," I rambled excitedly. If Mom was in on this with me, it would be so much easier to track Dad down," And, er, we have a huge English project due tomorrow, so I have to go at nine-"

Mom laughed, "Honey, did you know that I'm so very proud of you for trying out for the Black Sisterhood?" said Mom. I froze.

"Who told you?" I asked.

"Sophia. I saw her at Claire's not too long ago. Said you're one of the bravest she's ever met, and I couldn't agree more. So, you mean you have to go at nine for Task Three?" said Mom casually.

"Yeah," I started, but broke off, still shocked. First of all, Mom knew. Second of all, Sophia said I was one of the bravest people she's ever met?

"Er," I wondered if Mom knew I was pretending to be sick, "Er."

"Oh, right, I'm not bringing you any medications. It's not good to give medication to people who aren't really sick," continued Mom.

I gawked at her: "Can I please still stay home from school?" I asked hopefully, and to my great surprise and delight, Mom nodded.

"Get ready, Lex, today's a big day for both of us," said Mom with a determined look on her face, "Mission One for you is to complete Task Three. Mission Two is for both of us to find out the truth behind your father's workplace."

I nodded, but was still stunned. Never in my life had I thought this would ever happen...

It was eight thirty, and I was dressed and ready to go. The laboratory was a little ways from here, so Mom had volunteered to drive me. We told Dad we were going shopping together and would be back soon, but Dad hardly noticed. He was on the phone with someone again. Here's how our plan went: Mom would drive me to the laboratory and wait in the car until I came back out. We would then drive quietly back home, and not let Dad know we were back. We would hide our car behind a large tree, and wait for Dad to come out for his night shift. We then would follow him.

I was skittish and could tell Mom was too. We piled into the car, and drove off, me playing with my fingers anxiously, Mom humming to herself. I was about ready to burst with eagerness as Mom drove up to the lab. I gave her a quick kiss, took a deep breath, and got out of the car.

The laboratory was tremendous and I didn't know where I would need to go to meet Sophia, Cerise, and the scientists. I saw Mom take out her reading glasses and a book. She was waiting until I came back. We had agreed that if I wasn't back in an hour, she would come looking for me.

I was greeted by a jumpy Sophia and grinning Cerise. They collided with me just as I was about to enter and gave me a massive hug:

"Follow us, there's a special room for you," said Sophia, grabbed my hand and we ran off to the room. Or should I say the doom?

Cerise trailed behind us, occasionally stepping on my heels and muttering her apology. I could tell she was also volatile for me. The room we arrived in was massive with high ceilings and many murmuring scientists standing all around. They quickly hushed when they saw us enter the room.

Sophia clapped her hands and spoke in a loud voice: "Er, we don't want to make things too long, so without further ado, unless Lexie has any questions, let's begin!"

Everyone turned to me and my heart pounded even louder, drumming methodically against my sternum: "I think I'm fine," I muttered, looking down at my feet and folding my hands.

Sophia smiled gently and placed a hand on my shoulder. She steered me around to face her:

"Lexie, you'll do great. Everything's going to be okay, no matter what," she said, patting me on the back, "Just remember to breathe and be calm. Ten minutes is not too long."

I grinned back, legs and arms shaking. Cerise nudged me and I turned to face her: "Hey, quick tip. Don't fight your fears. Just ignore them. Turn them into something else in your head. Something funny and appealing, she said.

A beaming scientist with black hair that looked like a pudding bowl yanked my arm. He grinned, showing gleaming white teeth, and led me over to a reclining chair. A small white table filled with sharp needles and murky liquids stood by the chair. I gulped.

"Shall we begin?" said the scientist with an authentic British accent, "If the young lady is ready?"

I nodded, barely able to speak due to my unease. The scientists took about five minutes to prepare something. Butterflies fluttered in my stomach, and I felt slightly nauseated as a scientist filled a needle with liquid.

"Breathe, just breathe," said the scientist. I closed my eyes, taking deep breaths. The scientists took different needles and I felt a searing pain causing me to let out a small *ah!* before slipping away into some kind of bizarre dream.

I was standing in a vast field. The grass was yellowish and the sky overhead was cloudy and grey. I was wearing the same clothes, but was in a completely different location. I heard a raven let out a deep, rasping call and I sensed that something bad was coming my way.

I felt a sharp pain and looked down at my arm. A button saying "Escape" had been put into it.

All of a sudden I heard a piercing scream from behind me. A man wearing a black tux and a mask was pointing a gun at a few people tied into chairs. I gasped when I realized who was in those chairs: Mom, Dad, Carly, Sophia, Cerise, Bella, Ella, and Shella. Family and friends in danger; one of my fears.

The man roared at all the people to be quiet, flecks of spit flying from his mouth. Mom sobbed and the man raised his gun and shot her. An arc of blood shot from her body and she screamed, slumping down in her chair. Her head lolled back.

Dad yelled in rage and the man shot him, too. He took a sharp intake of breath, blood seeping from his stomach. He continued wheezing until he finally slumped just like Mom in his chair, dead.

It took all my willpower not to press the button on my hand as I began to weep helplessly. Carly fixed the man with a firm gaze and stuck out her tongue. The man sneered and shot her. She began to cry, screaming "Mommy, Daddy, I'm dying!" but her body didn't hold for much longer.

Bella, Ella, and Shella all tried to break free, but the ropes were tight and the man's gun was on the ready. BAM! BAM! BAM! He shot all three of them, and they died slower than the rest, but it was painful to watch. Bella shrieked, tears rolled down

Ella's cheeks, and Shella clutched her stomach, moaning.

The three of them soon collapsed in the chair and died. Sophia and Cerise were left. Sophia looked absolutely petrified as the man approached her, his gun out. BANG! BANG! He shot Sophia two times: in the head, and in the stomach.

She hunched over, and threw up. Blood ran from her mouth and her veins popped. She screamed in agony and began to die, still throwing up blood, her eyes rolling to the back of her head.

Cerise looked furious: "YOU! SON! OF! A-" BANG! She was interrupted when the man shot her in the leg. She clutched it in pain, bleeding and crying. The man looked slightly disappointed.

"Guess it takes two stones to kill a naughty lil' bird like you!" he bellowed, raised the gun, and shot Cerise in the heart. The bullet ripped open her skin and entered. She clutched her heart, eyes bulging, and fell to the ground, the ropes around her bursting, trying to crawl to freedom while gasping impotently. The man laughed malevolently and kicked her. She took her last breath of air and died.

I lowered to the ground, sobbing hysterically. I didn't notice that the man and all my dead loved ones had disappeared. I felt as if I had been shot in the heart, head, stomach, and leg. The pain was so profound. I felt my arm stretching to press the "Escape" button, but stopped myself when I noticed where I was.

I was suspended high up in the air on a rope as thin as a lock of hair. I was sitting on that rope, and when I looked down, I felt sick to my stomach and dizzy. Skyscrapers rose everywhere, and I threw up inside of my mouth. I leaned back slightly and went hurtling down. I grabbed onto the rope at the last moment, and pulled myself up, sweating and giddy.

When I looked down, I realized I had gotten higher up. I curled up into a tight ball, gasping for breath, stressed, icy sweat pouring down my forehead. I kept on getting higher up and higher up, afraid to look down. Unfortunately for me, I couldn't help it.

I screeched at the top of my lungs, nearly going hoarse and began to cry uncontrollably. I buried myself in my hands again, not realizing my surroundings had changed for the second time.

I was in a very tight, glass box that made my tiny amount of claustrophobia kick in. I was already having a little atrial fibrillation when things got even more disastrous. Thousands of spiders began to scuttle toward me, some big, some small, some medium-sized. I screamed, cried, vomited, slashed at them, getting my hand ready to press the button.

I then remembered what Cerise had told me. Turning spiders into something appealing was going to require rocket science, so I just decided to lay down and close my eyes.

I thought of the beach and nice things like summer vacation and ice cream. Getting my mind off the spiders was nice and it almost felt like a nice massage when I was off in Lalaland, forgetting about the hairy creatures.

A deep, booming voice suddenly filled the tank, counting off from ten and I felt a twinge of happiness. I couldn't count my chickens before they hatched, though. God knows what else could happen to me in the ten seconds I had left. But I survived, thankfully. The voice yelled "ZERO!" clamorously and I woke back up in the lab to cheers and applause.

I still felt nauseated on the inside, but brushed it off. Sophia and Cerise embraced me, confetti falling from hidden tiles in the ceiling. I had passed. I had survived Task Three.

CHAPTER SEVEN

"So, er, your mom knows about the Black Sisterhood now, right?" asked Sophia. We warmed up with some chamomile tea before going. My stomach was queasy and flashbacks of the fears persisted with an incessant demeanor.

"Yeah, she's chill with it," I answered, still trembling from all the memories of Task Three.

"Uh, can we do Task Four tomorrow? Right after school at Claire's in the ladies' restroom?" asked Sophia.

I nearly dropped my cup in surprise: "In the ladies' restroom at Claire's in broad daylight?" I questioned, thunderstruck.

Sophia shrugged and sipped her tea: "Your mom'll be there, and don't worry, the look isn't going to be too emo. I've already got the sketches in my notebook. Cerise, Bella, Ella, and Shella have seen the sketches, but they're excited to see it on you," she said.

Cerise nodded, smiling. She was unusually silent tonight, and I wondered why: "Er, sorry guys, but my mom's waiting for me," I said, my phone buzzing as Mom called me, "See you tomorrow at school."

"See you, Lexie!" cried Sophia after me, and Cerise waved genteely. I hurriedly waved, and rushed out the front doors. Mom greeted me with a smile.

"Hey, Mom, I passed!" I yelled, flinging the door open and giving Mom a huge hug, "It was the scariest experience of my life, but it was great overall!"

"Oh, good job, honey!" ejaculated Mom, squeezing me tightly, "I knew you'd be fine."

"No time to waste, Mom, it's ten thirty, Dad's ought to leave soon," I said, buckling up, "Let's go."

Mom nodded adamantly, put the key in the ignition, and we zoomed off into the inky night. The bare trees swayed menacingly above us, the wind howling like a pair of hungry coyotes. The moon shone brightly in the sky, peeking out behind one of the trees.

We finally arrived home and silently parked behind a large tree. We saw Dad coming out of the house, the moon reflecting off of his face in a malevolent way. Dad was holding the black bag he always carried with him whenever he went to work. We watched him load the bag into the back of the trunk, get into the driver's seat and roll out of the driveway.

We noiselessly followed him along the winding road. The drive was long, and my rear end was starting to get sore. Dad soon came to an abrupt halt and Mom stopped as well. We had arrived at a rundown gray building with a tiny wooden door in the corner. The building was filled with graffiti and spray paint.

"Doesn't look like a global networking company," I muttered under my breath, and Mom nodded her agreement. We parked the car behind Dad and crept out, hidden by the shadows. Dad heaved the bag out of the trunk with a grunt and set off to the door. I was acting on a hunch, and so I assumed, was Mom: Dad definitely had been lying to us.

We snuck in behind him on tiptoes, quiet as mice. I straightened my aching back and massaged my shoulders. The room was dim and musty, and reeked terribly. The ceiling was high up and windows had been carved into the walls, with one sheet of glass in them. Moon poured in through the windows, revealing the cobwebs all over the walls. Huge, wooden crates with black locks on them were piled all around the room.

Dad laid down the black bag and sighed. We heard a creaking noise and the lights came on. They were flickering and feeble. Mom and I dove behind one of the crates. We glimpsed from behind the wooden crate to see what was going on. An old lady with white hair hobbled out, supported by a tall man with broad shoulders. They came out of a back door etched and carved strategically on the floor.

They brought an abhorrent and utterly sickening smell with them. I guessed they had crawled out of the sewage pipes to get to this place. The old lady stretched her hand out and Dad handed her the bag. For someone so aged, she had a lot of strength but not enough. Gasping for breath, she handed it to the young man standing with her. He took an empty wooden crate from a corner, opened the bag, and poured the contents into the crate. I was shocked. Dad was in business with drug dealers.

"Thank you, Madam Kella and Sir Donald," said Dad, bowing nervously. The old lady nodded stoutly and the man saluted Dad.

"Until tomorrow!" said Madam Kella in a voice that sounded like creaky door hinges, desperately needing to be oiled.

"Yes, Madam Kella, until tomorrow," said Dad, genuflecting, "And you too, Mr. Donald."

The two drug dealers smiled coldly and the old lady limped back out, followed by the man. Dad looked giddy, but his fingers were shaking a bit.

"You forgot to pay me for tonight's delivery!" cried Dad, his voice breaking, 'Member, thousand dollars for every delivery."

"We agreed on nine hundred," said Sir Donald stiffly, "I know we are not the only ones you work with in this drug business of yours, so nine hundred should be plenty for you. How's the lie with your family going?"

"Those stupid cows know nothing," said Dad, waving his hand in the air, "In fact, it was I who forced my youngest daughter out of the house. Walked up to her in the middle of the night, holding a lighter in her face. Told her to go, told her to write that note. She left unwillingly, I pushed her out of the house. She won't be back anytime soon."

"Why?" sneered Sir Donald, "Why'd you push her out?"

"She's smart," replied Dad, "She'd break my secret before anyone else."

I felt faint. Mom and I waited until Sir Donald and Madam Kella left through the hole in the floor, and then stepped out from behind the crates.

Dad spun around, shocked: "Er, hi?" he said. Mom looked so mad, I could've sworn I saw steam erupting from her ears in puffy clouds of smoke. She came up to Dad and slapped him across the face. Blood trickled from his nose and he looked slightly ashamed of himself.

"You *sick bastard!* Is this all true? Looks like someone'll be talking to the damn police soon!" yelled Mom, and whipped out her phone, "Lex, dear, keep him on check."

"Yep, I said, looking my lying father in the eyes, "Consider yourself dead to me. You're no longer my father, Dad. Or should I say-"

"Who ever said I'll listen to you, cowards and stay here," sneered Dad, and Mom nodded at me.

My eyes flooded with tears. There was no second path to take.

Dad and Mom were both watching me, slightly apprehensive. I couldn't bring myself to do it. I told myself my Dad was a criminal and deserved a life sentence, but then a memory resurfaced.

It was my first Taekwondo class and I was dressed in an oversize dobok, excited but nervous. I was young back then and still lived in Pennsylvania. I had started with the beginners class, and my teacher, Master Chen was teaching me how to do a good kick. Master Chen told me right then and there, that my kicks came naturally. I had done my first ever kick with perfect technique and strength.

"Look, Mommy, Daddy!" I cried, rushing over to Mom and Dad, still barefoot, "My kicks come naturally!" I swung at them, sticking my tongue out, giggling uncontrollably.

"Woah there, Lex," said Dad, "Practice your kicks all you want, but we can't be your practice targets!" Dad, Mom, and I laughed together.

"What he said," said Mom goofily, but then her face expression turned serious and she clasped my hands in her hands, "I need you to understand that

no matter what, you never need to hurt your family. No matter what happens."

I nodded, not understanding how important this all was. Not knowing that someday I would most likely need to hurt a family member for our family's good...

"Do it, Lex, forget what I told you about hurting your family," Mom whispered in my ear. I looked at her, shocked. It was almost as if she could read my mind. I guess we were just really close.

Dad started looking nervous, but before he had the chance to escape, I growled, leapt up and swung at him.

"Alexis Torres, what are you doing?!" yelled Dad, "Is this some sort of game?"

"I'm sorry!" I cried, and slashed at Dad with my leg. Blood erupted from his mouth like a fountain, and one of his teeth fell out. He came crashing to the ground, unconscious before he even made contact with the hard floor.

"Okay, I'm calling the police, nice job," said Mom hurriedly, pressed a few buttons on her phone, and went into a corner to talk to the Parkersburg Police Station.

Everything around me went blurry. My father was lying on the ground, bleeding like crazy from the mouth, one of his teeth knocked out, and unconscious. Let alone the fact that he most likely had a major concussion, too. And I had caused that with one swift kick. I began to sob, despair clouding up my brain.

"Father, I'm so sorry!" I cried, petting Dad's arm, "A-a-after Task Three, I c-c-can't see you or anyone I love hurt! I-I-I know y-you've done s-s-some bad s-stuff, but w-we can forgive and f-f-forget. I-I-I'm sure you l-l-love Carly, and o-only mean t-t-the best f-f-for all of us!"

Mom was watching me, a heartbroken look crossing her face: "Lex, I'm so sorry!" she cried, running up to me, "Your father is a crook who deserves jail time, and kicks in the face every single day! I know he's your father, but he's a stranger and miscreant to *me*."

I could barely breathe. I saw stars, and blackness was closing in on me. My head hurt, and my body collapsed into Mom's knees, still crying, half-unconscious, half-conscious. I saw blue and red lights reflecting off the building walls and sirens wailing loudly outside.

Police cars and ambulances had come. The police stormed in, guns raised, their faces set. I screamed, crying, snot and tears and blood running down my face, head still pounding.

The police put Dad in handcuffs and a few doctors laid him onto stretchers. I reached out my hand, and Mom struggled to force me back, but there was no stopping me now.

I ran up to Dad, sirens howling in the background, police and doctors yelling for me to step away. I ignored them. The only thing that mattered right now was my Dad.

I wanted to yell for them to be quiet, to let me talk to Dad again, but I couldn't bring myself to. My throat was as dry as sandpaper, and blood, sweat, and tears encapsulated my face. I leaned in to Dad, and could've sworn I saw his eyes flicker open and a smile spread across his face.

"I love you, Dad, and I didn't mean for this to happen. I want you to know I will never forgive you for what you did, but you are my father and I love you with all my heart. I hope everything will be okay," I murmured, and kissed Dad on the forehead.

"I love you, Lex," he croaked in a quiet voice, then went stiff and his eyes closed. Panic flooded through me.

"What just happened?" I asked, heart pounding. Mom rushed up to the stretcher Dad was in. A doctor reached out to feel his pulse and went pale.

"Goodness," said the doctor, "He has died. The cause is unknown."

"Take him to the Institution of Forensic Pathology," said one of the police, "Guess karma hit the man hard."

I felt like an overflowing cup. But I wasn't overflowing with water. I was overflowing with the deepest grief I had ever felt. I collapsed to my knees, sobbing, and Mom tried to help me up, but I slapped her hand away. She didn't understand. *She* wasn't crying, *she* didn't feel like jumping off the Empire State Building, *she* wasn't thinking it was her fault Dad had died.

A few doctors came up to me and tried to console me, but I screeched at them to leave, and wept even harder. Everyone was talking in low, strained voices. The doctors loaded Dad into the back of the ambulance, and sped off. The police tried to control the situation, but failed miserably. The doctors who were left ran around, clutching their hair, muttering under their breath. This was the first time something like this had ever happened.

"Ma'am, you and your daughter have to leave immediately," said an officer, "There are two cars parked outside. If one of them is yours, go now."

"When will be informed of the cause of my husband's death?" rasped Mom irately, "I've got too much on my plate at the moment."

"He is being taken to the Institution of Forensic Pathology," replied the officer, "You will be informed tomorrow morning."

"Okay, Lex, we have to go," said Mom in a voice choked with tears. She grabbed my hand and led me away. I refused to give in, but finally gave up. I let Mom drag me away, both of us weeping. We piled into the car, and that night, I only remembered feeling traumatized and emotionally disturbed.

I cried myself to sleep, continuously waking up to realize that I might have killed Dad. His life had been given into cruel hands, and those hands could've been mine. Twice during the night I walked into Mom's room. She was hunched over a photograph of her and Dad, surrounded by boxes of tissues. Mom may have been upset at Dad, but the death of a loved one always brings out our most despondent selves.

During lunch, I filled the Black Sisterhood in on what had happened. They all mourned along with me, and showed their respect. I never thought I'd actually find someone as caring as them.

Sophia offered to postpone Task Four, but I turned her generous offer down: "The sooner, the better," I said, "I don't think Mom will be at Claire's after school, but we'll see."

"Wait, so, when do you find out, er, the cause of, um, you know, your Dad's, er-" stuttered Ella, squirming uncomfortably. She clearly felt bad for asking.

"It's alright," I said, tears trickling down my face. I quickly rubbed them away, "I'll know when I get home from school, well, after Task Four that is. Unless, Mom's in Claire's, which I highly doubt."

Word had spread around school that Dad had died, and everyone paid their respects to me wherever I went. The teachers excused me from homework for the rest of the week, and even Midge gave her condolences.

The bus driver noticed I was peculiarly quiet that day, and pestered me to tell him what was wrong. I didn't want to, though. Telling *him* out of all people about Dad's death would make me look like an attention seeker.

"Yer know I'm not going ter waste me time driving yer ter Claire's if yer don't tell me," said the bus driver, wagging a finger in my face, "I ain' joking he' yer know."

"Just drama at school," I mumbled, as the bus driver pulled up to Claire's, "I'll figure it out, but I've never liked being involved in drama."

"Me neitha," answered the bus driver, laughing heartily, "Gosh, m'lady, yer got me scared fer a second ther'. Though' yer fatha died or somethin'."

I tried not to listen to these last words as tears gathered in my eyes. I bounced off the bus steps and as soon as I stepped into Claire's, I knew something was wrong. Mom was crying into a napkin, and Sophia was soothing her.

She looked up at me with red eyes: "Lex!" she yelled, "Y-y-your father- well, I'll let Sheriff Morber explain. Go ahead, Sheriff."

Sheriff Morber turned to me with a grave expression: "I'll make it quick, Alexis," he said, "We searched the house. Apparently, your father has been getting blackmailed by someone who calls themselves the Cloaked One. This Cloaked One forced your father into a drug business and into kicking Carly out of the house. The Cloaked One also threatened to slit all your throats in front of your father if he didn't fulfill the tasks."

I covered my mouth with my hand: "So what happened next?" I asked, dreading the answer.

Sheriff Morber sighed and Mom burst into tears once more: "See, your father wanted to be an innocent man. He told the Cloaked One that the delivery he made last night would be his last one. He lied to the people he saw last night, told them he would be back the next night, but planned to have no such thing happen."

"And?" I questioned. Sheriff Morber looked even more grim than he had before.

"We found this last blackmail on your father's phone. And, it's not pretty, let me tell you that right away," continued Sheriff Morber, "Your father didn't see the blackmail yet, but the Cloaked One said he would gruesomely murder your father. What your father didn't know is that the Cloaked One placed a killing chip in him. Said it was just a tracking chip, but really, it was a killing chip. The button was pressed at the last minute."

"Wait, what?" I asked, puzzled, "So my father has been getting blackmailed and threatened, right? And then he said he wanted to be innocent, right? And this Cloaked One put a killing chip into him and killed him at the last moment, oh no."

"Other than the obvious reason, is everything alright, Miss Torres?" asked Sheriff Morber.

I shook my head, going pallid: "Roberto and Olga were interacting with the Cloaked One, and he killed them through killing chips," I said, "My father was next. Don't you see a pattern here, Sheriff? And to add to that, I always see a cloaked figure outside this abandoned house not far from mine."

Now the Sheriff went pale: "You mean, er, the House of Doom?" he asked, "Do you know what happened there?" Mom tried to hush him, but I shook my head and beckoned for him to go on.

"A family was killed there thirty years ago. They were all slaughtered with an axe. It was a family of three, and nobody survived. The killer escaped, and for all we know, could still be alive. It could be the Cloaked One, or the original killer could have passed it onto the Cloaked One," reasoned the Sheriff.

I was shocked. That's why Task Five would be so utterly frightening. Chills went up my spine at the mere thought of it.

Sophia clapped her hands: "Okay, Sheriff Morber, thank you for ruining any chance of us having good dreams tonight," she said, and the Sheriff sighed, "C'mon, now, Lexie, time for Task Four."

I followed her to the ladies' restroom, but couldn't help thinking about the Cloaked One. I felt he or she was so close, yet so far away....

CHAPTER EIGHT

"Voila!" cried Sophia, spinning my chair around to face the mirror. My hair had been straightened and cut to my shoulders with blonde highlights around the corners. Lip gloss was smeared over my mouth, shining with an inexplicable effulgence.

"Wow, Sophia," I said, looking down at my flawless cuticles, "This looks great!"

"Oh, I'm not done yet," answered Sophia, holding up five bags teeming with clothes, "I hit twenty of my favorite stores some time ago, and bought you tons of clothing. You're expected to wear it from here on out."

"Oh," I said, and my face fell, "Okay, then, as long as it's comfortable and not too over the top."

Sophia chuckled and handed me the five bags: "It's comfortable, but it may seem a little extreme at first. You'll get used to it, though," she said.

"You said I'm expected to wear it from here on out," I said, "Does that mean I have to change into an outfit now?"

Sophia nodded animatedly: "Pick out anything you want," she cried and turned away to let me change. I made my way to the corner, pulling a few random articles of clothing out of the bag.

I was disgusted. These clothes looked like something a gang member would wear, and would not look good on me. I pulled on a pair of fishnet tights with repugnance, and snatched a glance at the mirror.

Next up was a black skirt that was shorter than any shorts my Mom would ever have allowed me to wear. A hissing cobra was sewn into the left side of the skirt and a roaring tiger was sewn into the right side. I threw on a short, white blouse that revealed my belly button. I tried to pull my skirt up to cover it, but it was designed to repudiate me.

I saw Sophia bouncing up and down on the balls of her feet out of the corner of my eye. She was eager to see how the new clothes looked on me. I gently put on a black leather jacket and adjusted the pre-rolled up sleeves.

"Er, I think I'm done," I said, and Sophia turned around. She surveyed me with a grin until her eyes dropped to my feet. The leader's face fell in disappointment.

"You have to change into new shoes, Lexie, not keep your old Skechers. They're too worn-out and childish," she said, pursing her lips, "Put on your new faux snakeskin boots."

"Faux?" I asked, "They're not real?"

"Oh, no, let me clarify something," said Sophia, "Using real animal skin for clothing or accessories is a big no-no. It's cruel and terrible, and anyone who does it should be ashamed of themselves. We only use faux animal skin boots."

I couldn't have agreed more as I pulled on the faux snakeskin boots. They hurt my heel, and were tight and unpleasant to wear. I could already feel a blister forming and blood seeping through.

"Er, for Task Five, can I wear sneakers?" I questioned.

"Yeah, but not your old ones," responded Sophia and unlocked the bathroom door, "Meet me at the House of Doom tomorrow at eleven o'clock at night. There we will hold Task Five."

"Sounds good," I said, but it did not sound good in the least bit. I was more scared than I had ever been before in my life. For all I knew, I would see the Cloaked One there tomorrow night. And what if he chose to enter the house?

Jaws dropped the next day at school everytime I walked by in the hallways or classrooms. People complimented me and even Ava who I still hadn't gotten a chance to apologize to, accoladed me:

"You look great, Lexie," she said, "Good luck on Task Five tonight."

"Ava, I'm really sorry about what happened between us," I said, "I know what I did was wrong, and-"

Ava interrupted me with a large hug that muffled my speech, and I smiled broadly on the inside and outside: "*I'm* sorry, Lexie," said Ava, looking genuinely apologetic, "What I said was unacceptable, and those words never should've come out of my mouth. I hope you can forgive me, because I've already forgiven you."

"Of course, Ava, I appreciate your apology," I said, and we hugged again. I saw Cerise throw us a wistful look, but quickly looked away when she saw that I had noticed her.

"Anyways, see you around, Lexie!" cried Ava, and ran away to her locker to get her textbooks for her next class. Cerise came over, limping slightly, her face scratched in a few places.

"Cerise, are you okay?" I asked, noticing her bruises. She waved it off:

"I just fell off a tree last night. It was dark and I couldn't see the next branch I meant to jump down to," said Cerise, looking away, "What's going on between you and Ava?"

"Oh, er, we were just making up for the fight we had where I punched her, remember that?" I said, chuckling.

"Tis in my memory lock'd, and you yourself shall keep the key of it," responded Cerise, quoting William Shakespeare.

"Why were you climbing a tree?" I asked, pondering the thought. It was unlike the Cerise I knew to go climbing up a tree at night without anyone to spot her.

Cerise went a grotesque shade of green: "You can't tell Sophia," she said, "Promise."

"I promise," I said, and Cerise sighed, looking away once more.

"Well, you know Sophia's dating Dillon, right?" said Cerise and I nodded mournfully.

"Were you spying on them or something?" I asked, and Cerise shrugged her shoulders.

"Kinda," she continued, "I mean, Sophia was gloating that she and Dillon were going to hang out last night at her house, so I decided to prank them. I crept up onto a tree next to Sophia's house with a pair of binoculars. I saw them watching a movie and decided to use a paintball gun to shoot them. It would've been hilarious, if only I hadn't fallen off and injured myself."

"Injured yourself?" I asked in a concerned voice.

"Nothing too bad," replied Cerise, "I just twisted my wrist, sprained my ankle and got a few bruises here and there."

"Oh, I'm so sorry," I said, and Cerise laughed, shaking her head.

"That's not the scariest part though, Lexie," she added, "It was *him*."

"Him?" I asked, confused.

"Yes, him," said Cerise, "The Cloaked One. He shook the tree and I fell off. Thought it was just the wind at first, but then I saw him running away into the forest beyond Sophia's house."

"Who's to say it's a he?" I asked, and Cerise shrugged.

"Anyways, see you tonight for Task Five," said Cerise, thumping me on the back and turning to leave.

"Wait, I haven't seen Shella yet today," I said, and Cerise turned back to talk to me, "Is she okay?"

"Poor thing is sick," said Cerise, "She has a temperature of forty Celsius. She's still coming to Task Five, though."

"No, tell her to rest," I said, "A temperature like that, that's hapless for her. She can skip out on Task Five if she'd like to stay home and rest. I don't mind as long as she feels better."

Cerise smiled: "Thanks for being considerate to her, Lexie," said Cerise and left to her next class.

When I came home, Mom was sitting in the kitchen, resting her head in her trembling hands. A bouquet of fresh roses was lying next to her.

"Mom, is that from Albert?" I asked before I could stop myself.

"We'll talk about Albert later," said Mom, her jaw quivering, "See for yourself." I sensed it was something bad as I picked up the bouquet of roses and looked inside.

A letter scrawled in hasty handwriting lay there. I screamed when I read the letter (which consisted of letters cut from newspapers to disguise the anonymous writer's handwriting), and dropped it to the ground: I will come for you next- Cloaked One

"Mom, the Cloaked One killed Roberto, Olga, and Dad. What does he want from you?" I asked, quivering, "Why is the Cloaked One on such a huge killing spree?"

"How would I know?" asked Mom, "You see the Cloaked One every night by the House of Doom. I'm betting it's the person who killed that poor family."

"Mom, you have to show this to the police," I said, and Mom nodded.

"I already called them. They put cameras up all around the house," she said, "Gave me extra protection locks and curtains for free."

"So, you're going to be okay?" I asked, and reached out to hold Mom's hands. She looked up at me, her bottom lip trembling, eyes watering.

"Everything's going to be alright," said Mom in a choked voice, and began sobbing into my shirt.

"Er, Mom, sorry but, can we talk about something I noticed on the first day of school?" I said, and Mom looked up with snot and tears dribbled all down her front.

"Sure," said Mom, looking down with a guilty expression.

"So, you know how Carly and I were waiting for you to pick us up by the football field?" I began, and Mom sighed. "Er, I saw you with Albert. I saw him give you the money and I saw your guys' romantic relationship. I was heartbroken that you cheated on Dad, but more shocking news came along. Turns out Albert is Dillon's father."

"Dillon?" questioned Mom, puzzled.

"Sophia's boyfriend. We, erm, went to the movies together sometime ago. Sophia, Cerise, Dillon, and me. Dillon's motorcycle broke or something, so his Dad had to pick him up," I explained, and Mom groaned.

"I'm so sorry, honey. I've been meaning to tell you, but I couldn't bring myself to. I *knew* you'd be extremely anguished, but you would find out sooner or later," said Mom, and I felt great pity for her. She was going through a hard time, and I couldn't blame her for losing control once in a while.

"It's okay, Mom. I understand," I said, and Mom's face lit up. We hugged for a brief moment, before I pulled back with a question.

"Is everything alright?" asked Mom worriedly, and I nodded.

"I just have a question," I responded, "How'd you two meet? He did tell me he saw you at Claire's."

"Oh, did he? Well, he's not lying, no. We did indeed meet at Claire's on my first day on the job," prattled Mom, "He told me I had a beautiful smile, and we made out that evening. It was after you had left already, of course. Told me he'd swing by tomorrow morning and I gave him my address. Albert's quite the marvel and I'd like to keep seeing him."

"If that's what makes you happy," I said, but suddenly felt a spurn of outrage in my blood, "If you'll excuse me, I have Task Five tonight and must go get ready."

Time passed rapidly. I found myself at the door, heart thumping uncontrollably. Mom wished me luck as I left, but I ignored her. I understood her troubles, but her words angered me.

The walk to the House of Doom was short, but frightening. With every step, my heart pounded louder and louder. I kept on hearing sounds and what sounded like footsteps behind me, only to realize it was squirrels scurrying through piles of dead leaves.

Sophia was standing by the House of Doom, flanked by Bella and Ella. She approached me with outstretched arms and gave me a hug:

"Hey, Lexie!" she cried, "Er, so Shella isn't going to be here tonight-"

"I know," I said, anxiously bouncing on my toes, "Where's Cerise?"

"She'll be joining us soon," said Sophia, "She's a little late, but we can excuse her. So remember, six minutes per floor. Five floors. Six multiplied by five is thirty. You'll be spending half an hour in the House of Doom. As you progress through the house, we will be notifying you. Once six minutes has passed on the first floor, I will text you. Once six minutes has passed on the second floor, I will text you again. And so on, and so forth."

"Erm, so can I just stand in one spot for six minutes?" I asked.

"No, we will attach a camera to you. You must move freely around the floor and explore every room. It is scary, but I have confidence in you, Lexie. Once your thirty minutes are up, you immediately have to come out. At any given time you may call quits, but you will fail the task," said Sophia, hooking a body camera onto my shirt.

Cerise suddenly ran up behind us, panting heavily. Her face was flushed, and her hands were stained in blood: "I'm so sorry I'm late," she said, and we all eyed her hands with a mounting suspicion.

"Guys, what's wrong?" she asked, confused, "Can we please just start Task Five? I didn't come all this way for nothing."

"Erm, Cerise, the walk from your house to the House of Doom is fairly short," said Bella, and we all nodded our agreement. Something was definitely wrong.

"Guys, look, can I please explain later?" said Cerise in an agitated tone of voice, "Lexie is waiting for Task Five to start." She caught my eye and flashed a wink at me. I wondered what that wink meant.

"Cerise's right," said Ella, "Lexie's got the camera attached to her and I think she's ready to go inside the house. Are you ready, Lexie?"

My shoulders stiffened. I nodded my head and Sophia grinned. She pried open the old, mossy door with a light push. Ella patted my arm as I stared up at the House of Doom. It looked terrifying.

My breath caught in my lungs and I fought a battle inside. I could drop out, but then regret it forever. Going inside would be seemingly much easier.

"You sure you're ready for this, Lexie?" asked Sophia and I nodded once more.

"Atta girl," she said, and handed me a flashlight with a large grin, "We don't want you tripping over anything or getting hurt since it's dark outside. Go on in. We wish you the best of luck. This night may determine your whole life, so tread carefully."

"How will it determine my whole life?" I questioned, feeling my heart rise into my Adam's Apple as I looked up at the forsaken house.

"The Black Sisterhood can get you far in life," replied Sophia with a quick wink, "Now, c'mon, get in there, Lexie. May luck shine upon you like a bright ray of sunlight."

Icy sweat gathered at my forehead and dripped down my face. Without turning around, I clicked on my flashlight and stepped into the house. Ella closed the door behind me. My heart began to pummel against my chest harder than ever. Layers upon layers of dust muffled my footsteps and knocked over chairs and tables surrounded the house. Stale, crimson blood was dried on the wooden walls. A few shattered pictures in their frames were scattered across the floor.

"Oh my goodness," I whispered, gazing around in perturbation. I made my way to the first room, which looked like it had been a living room. Knocked over chairs, tables, sofas, and a destroyed grand piano in the corner. I proceeded to the next room which was the bathroom. A piece of the sink spattered in blood lay below my feet and it appeared a member of the family had been showering when they were killed. A couple of minutes later, a message appeared on my phone from Sophia. I was ready to go to the next floor.

I advanced through three more floors before something strange dawned on me. The family who had been killed was a family of only three. However, there was blood everywhere. I moaned lightly and clutched a rotting chair. It broke beneath my fingers.

The fifth floor was the scariest. All the bedrooms were there, and broken-down beds littered the floor. So did nightstands, closets, cabinets, and more. In one room, a framed photograph of a young girl and her mother had been fractured. A large cross had been drawn over it with blood. I thought I heard footsteps behind me. That made me feel even more mortified.

The sixth floor was coming up next. It was nothing too special. Just many storage rooms and an attic where bloody boxes were piled in a corner. Had someone been killed in the attic?

That's when I saw something that scared me half to death. Fresh blood was flecked all over a grimy photo of a man and woman smiling by a beach. Fresh blood. Not thirty-year old blood. Fresh blood. I whipped out my phone and snapped a picture. I had been doing this with everything that seemed suspicious.

At last, a text arrived on my phone. In all capital letters and with an abundance of exclamation points, Sophia told me that I was finished and was an official member of the Black Sisterhood. I looked out the window and saw the Black Sisterhood celebrating. I also saw the Cloaked One standing a little ways behind them. He bowed his head to me and ran for the hills. And that's also when I got a notification on my phone that would change my life forever...

CHAPTER NINE

Two minutes had passed since this news article was posted. The police had entered the house to find a little boy huddled in the corner, crying.

I sprinted out of the house, but wasn't met by cheers. The Black Sisterhood had gotten the notification, too. Sophia looked up at me with wide eyes:

"Do you think it could've been the Cloaked One?" she asked, and I shook my head.

"I just saw the Cloaked One a few minutes ago standing behind you guys. He bowed his head and dashed away. That house is a forty-five minute drive from here, and I assume the forest is where he resides. It was probably just some lunatic with a knife," I responded.

"Anyways, welcome to the Black Sisterhood," said Sophia, "We will hold the blood exchange tomorrow at my house at nine at night. I'll text you my address right now." Sophia swiftly typed something and my phone buzzed, but I couldn't check it right now. A more pressing matter was on our hands.

"It's the Black Sisterhood's job to solve mysteries and bring justice to the world, right?" I asked, ferociously jabbing my finger into the air, "I am an official member of the Black Sisterhood. I demand we now go to my house and watch the live interview. God knows what we'll hear there."

"I agree," said Cerise, stepping up, "Lex is with us now. She will obviously survive the blood exchange if she could handle everything else, so she's our sister now. Her word counts. Let's stay at her house for the night and watch the live interview. Will that be okay with your Mom, Lex?"

The sound of Cerise calling me Lex was music to my ears. I grinned: "Yes, she'll be thrilled to have you guys over. She'll also be happy I made it in," I replied.

We all ran a short distance to my house and barged in. Mom was sitting on the couch, watching the live interview. She turned around with a start at our clamorous entrance: "How'd it go, Lex? Did you make it in?" she asked.

"Yes, Lex made it in," said Sophia, "But can we please watch the live interview immediately, Mrs. Torres?" Mom nodded with a confused expression and scooted over to give us space on the couch. Bella and Ella sat on the floor and Cerise, Sophia, and I sat on the couch.

There was a short commercial break and we all turned to Cerise: "Why were your hands bloody and why did you have to run such a long distance?" interrogated Sophia with furrowed eyebrows.

"I was visiting Shella, and as you guys know, her house is pretty far from here. She was so sick, it was crazy. Poor thing. On the way, I tripped over a branch and scraped my hands. I swear that that's all there is to it," said Cerise. We believed her. She looked genuine, and Shella was very sick. There was no denying it.

The news came back on and all of our attention immediately snapped back to the television. The boy was sitting in a chair facing a police officer, shaking with tears of fright and trauma.

"It's okay, Archer, we'll figure this out," the officer was saying. The boy, Archer, was shaking like a thin leaf in brutal wind.

Snot ran down his face, and he was hiccuping and sobbing. The officer patted him: "Shall we begin the investigation with you, Archer?" asked the police in a gentle tone.

"Y-y-yes," said the boy in a trembling voice.

"Okay, can you please tell me what happened, Archer?" said the police officer, taking out a notepad and pen.

"A cloaked man barged in with a knife. Mommy tried to stab him with a kitchen knife, but he got to her first. Then, Daddy tried to help but the man stabbed him in the back. My older sister, Ava, ran out and he threw the bloody knife in her stomach. I was hiding in the laundry room and he didn't notice me. He wrote something on the wall in Mommy's blood, but I didn't see what it was. I was too scared to do anything, for fear that he would come again," said Archer, still shaking, tears flowing bellicosely down his face.

"What were your parents and sister doing at the time of the attack?" asked the officer, jotting down notes in his notepad.

"Mommy was cooking dinner, Daddy was reading a book, and Ava was trying on new clothes in her room," answered Archer.

"Why were you all up so late and why was your mother cooking dinner so late at night?" questioned the officer.

"We were taking a late night walk and decided to come home and eat dinner later than usual," replied Archer, "We were going to go to bed right after, but then you know-" He broke off in tears, rocking back and forth in his chair and moaning hysterically.

The police officer remained calm as ever: "It is probably the Cloaked One," he said, and I shared a meaningful look with the Black Sisterhood, "Yet there is still an ongoing investigation. We will have a SWAT team break into your house and see what has been written on the wall."

"There will be no need to use a SWAT team," said Archer, "The door is busted open. You can't find fingerprints, though, because the man was completely covered. Gloves, cloak, trench coat, and all."

"Thank you for the feedback, Archer," said the officer.

The news channel switched back to a reporter, wearing a concerned countenance: "Well, that is quite the story. If anyone has any information on this, please feel free to call 304-897-6457 immediately," she said, "Up next, world record broken for.."

The news reporter droned on, but I turned back to the Black Sisterhood with an uneasy feeling in my stomach: "Guys, we need to call that number and tell them. What if the Cloaked One has an apprentice or someone doing the dirty work for him?" I asked.

"I agree," said Ella, "We'll inform Shella about this once she gets better." I picked up my phone, dialed the number, and put the call on speaker. A man with a deep, booming voice answered:

"Hello, this is Officer Barnes," the man said, "How can I help you?"

"We have information concerning the attack tonight," I replied, "The boy assured the officer on the interview that the killer was the Cloaked One. The Cloaked One's place of residence is most likely the woods or the House of Doom itself. That place is about forty minutes from my house on car, but I saw the Cloaked One by the House of Doom like I do every night. Our guess is that the one I saw tonight is a prankster dressed up, or the Cloaked One has some kind of apprentice."

"By our, who do you mean?" asked the officer, "And what were you doing so late at the House of Doom?"

"Completing Task Five for the Black Sisterhood," I answered, "I saw him through the window. He bowed slightly to me and sprinted off. He was standing a little ways away from the Black Sisterhood, but they didn't notice him."

"Okay, I'm assuming you made it in?"

"Yes, Officer Barnes. Just some information I'd think you'd want to know."

"Thank you, this information will prove very useful in the investigation. Have a wonderful night," said the officer.

"Likewise," I replied, and hung up. I turned back to the Black Sisterhood with wide eyes, "Well, they'll do what they can, but I won't rest until we figure this all out."

Cerise smiled, and put her hand out. I put my hand out, too, and so did the rest of the Black Sisterhood. We cheered three times, and waved our hands in the air in a circular motion. Kind of like a secret Black Sisterhood handshake.

"Guys, should we rest now?" offered Bella, and the rest of us agreed.

"There's five of us. Three people can sleep on the floor, and someone can sleep with me in my bed. Not to sound weird or anything," I said.

"I like sleeping on the floor," said Ella, "Bella and I can sleep on the floor."

"Yeah, I can sleep on the floor, too," proffered Sophia, "Lex probably has a big bed, so there'll be enough room for both of you."

"Yeah," I said, yawning and stretching, "Let's go, guys." I bid Mom good-night, and the five of us trooped up the stairs. Sophia, Bella, and Ella laid out blankets and pillows and collapsed onto the floor, exhausted.

I brushed my teeth, noticing that Cerise was taking great care in not messing up the bedsheets as she climbed into the bed. I spit out the toothpaste, and turned around, chuckling.

"It's fine, you don't have to worry about the state of the bedsheets," I said, "They'll get messy during the night anyways. I kick when I sleep, so just warning you."

"Okay," replied Cerise, and I flicked the lights off. The moon cast an uncanny glow on the bed, drowning it in some kind of unforgiveness and despair. Cerise sat beside my lamp which poured red light all over her. I quickly turned it off and scrambled into bed next to Cerise, trying to keep a fair distance so it didn't appear intimate.

Cerise turned towards me: "Sophia was right," she murmured, and I looked around, puzzled, "You are special. The Black Sisterhood is the perfect place for you, and I'm glad you made it in."

"Same," I said, "It's great to hang out with you guys."

"I know I was a jerk at first," said Cerise, "And I'm sorry about that. My greatest weakness is being bad at accepting the fact that change happens."

"It's okay," I uttered, and everything went silent. I was about to turn back around, when Cerise grabbed me by the shoulder and pulled me in. She smelled like cocoa, licorice, and God's garden.

And as I lay with Cerise that night, I felt my heart flutter. This was me, and no one could take the fact that I am myself away from me. I loved Cerise, and Cerise loved me. Cerise was a like a shadow. She wouldn't abandon me even in times of darkness. I knew that. I knew that because she told me, and her word meant the world. So did she herself.

When Cerise and I awoke, Sophia and the others had already gone downstairs. It was nine in the morning, so I supposed we weren't going to school today. Cerise and I went down the stairs, holding hands. Everyone gaped at us, and Sophia smiled.

"Did you think I was asleep?" she asked slyly, "I saw you two last night. Congrats, guys."

Mom grinned at me, tears of joy shining in her eyes. All of a sudden, the doorbell rang and Mom hurried out of the kitchen to answer it.

Cerise and I settled down at the table next to the others. But when I saw who had rung the doorbell, my jaw dropped to the floor. Tears ran down my eyes, and I sprinted to squeeze Carly into the tightest hug I had ever given anyone.

She was as pale and thin as a skeleton, and her cheekbones were sunken in. Her eyes were dull and her hair was dirty. Her face shone as I embraced her tightly.

Mom was crying and hugging Carly, mascara running down her face: "Oh, dear God, Carly," she sobbed, "I thought something bad had happened to you. I thought the Cloaked One had come for you."

"You probably don't know who that is, Car," I said, and Carly shook her head.

"I was here in Parkersburg hiding the whole time. I occasionally peeked through people's' windows and saw the news," said Carly, "Erm, sorry to burst your bubble, but I think it's better if we kick Dad out of the house."

"We know he worked for a drug business and kicked you out of the house, Car," I said, "But the Cloaked One blackmailed him to do all of that, and then later killed him."

"Dad's dead?" asked Carly, looking appalled.

"Yeah," said Mom, and Carly burst into tears, "Sorry, honey. I think you should go wash up and eat something. God knows what's going on with you right now."

"O-o-okay," said Carly in a voice choked with tears, and she sprinted up the stairs, still bawling. Now that she understood it wasn't Dad's fault, it was much harder to realize. I knew because I had felt the same way.

"Let's turn on the news," said Mom, getting the remote control, "See what the update is on the killing case. Wonder what was written on the wall in that poor woman's blood."

I sat down at the table, and poured myself a glass of juice. Cerise took a cinnamon roll and smiled affectionately at me as I looked at her. A sudden scream erupting from Ella's throat drew our attention to the television.

The news reporter was back, talking feverishly. A picture of all the people killed in the attack was next to her. Ella had dropped her milk glass, and her eyes were glued to an older girl holding Archer by the shoulders.

"She must be his older sister," I said, "The one he described. Ava." It had suddenly dawned on me. Ava had been killed. The Ava I knew from school. My eyes watered. Right after Ava and I had made amends, she and her parents were murdered so gruesomely.

"Oh my goodness," said Bella, and Ella began to sob so hard, I couldn't hear the news reporter at all. Bella led Ella out of the room, trying to solace her.

Sophia was covering her mouth with her hand, and Cerise looked whiter than a paper fresh from the printer, "Guys, it's terrible what happened to Ava. But, look at the television screen," said Cerise.

All of our heads turned to the screen, and a piercing scream arose from Mom's mouth. The writing on the wall had been discovered. Ava's body, Archer's Mom's body, and Archer's Dad's body all lay beside the wall where something was written in red, rather fresh blood.

"It appears to be some sort of cipher," the news reporter was saying, "The cipher itself is unknown, but we have more news. Late last night, a member of the Black Sisterhood called and revealed some alarming information..."

Sophia whipped out her phone and took a picture of the bloody wall before the image on the screen disappeared, "C'mon, guys," she said. Bella and Ella had re-entered the room, and were staring open-mouthed at the screen.

"Are we going to decipher the code or not?" said Cerise, and we all leapt to our feet, "Shella's house has a special computer room. She might still be sick, but she'll let us use it. We'll figure out what type of code it is, and then decode it."

I stuffed my feet into warm boots, and Cerise opened the door wide. We all filed out, and ran off in the direction of Shella's house. The run was long, but we were all persistent to get there and figure out what message the Cloaked One had left behind.

Sophia, Cerise, and I made it to the house first. Shella's house was squat and rather run-down. A snobby boy with blonde hair opened the door when we knocked. Bella and Ella ran up behind us, panting and clutching a stitch in their sides.

"How can I help you?" he drawled, "I'm Shella's cousin and staying with her for some time while her parents are out an' about for work. I'm a legal guardian, don't fret."

"Shella's cousin, nice to meet you," I said, "We're here to see Shella in person. To decipher what the Cloaked One wrote on the wall in Archer's Mom's blood."

"I'm sorry, the Cloaked One?" said Shella's cousin. Spit flew from his mouth as he spoke, "Who is that?"

"Never you mind," I replied, bewildered that he didn't have a clue who the Cloaked One was, "Please just let us in."

"I know it's the Black Sisterhood behind ya, but who are *you*?" he asked, sneering down at me.

"Alexis Torres. I'm a new member of the Black Sisterhood. Let us in now," I responded, getting slightly agitated.

Shella's cousin didn't move a muscle. Sophia snapped angrily at him. He still didn't budge.

"Move out of the damn way, Charlie," said a raspy voice behind Shella's cousin who turned around indignantly. The five of us slipped past, and gave Shella a big hug.

She coughed, but looked pleased to see us, "Hey guys, sorry 'bout my cousin, Charlie," she said, "He can be quite the nuisance sometimes." Charlie rolled his eyes and stomped away.

"We need to use your computer room now," said Sophia in an urgent tone, "Did you hear the news this morning?"

"With my parents gone and Charlie here, I'm not allowed to do anything," replied Shella, rocking back and forth on her feet. There was something different about her. She looked almost as dirty as Carly, and smelled like tobacco.

"Has Charlie been treating you well, Shella?" asked Ella, "You don't look too good."

"Charlie's always smoking and I can't avoid it. His cooking is garbage and he only gives me the scraps," said Shella, "I've been sick a lot."

"Stay at my house, Shella," offered Sophia, "You're welcome anytime, and Lex can knock Charlie out if he objects."

"Thanks, Sophia," said Shella, "I am in need of more rest, but y'all can head down to the computer room. Tell me what's goin' on later. When's Lex's blood thing? Did she even make it in?"

"Yeah," I announced proudly, "Thank you, Shella. You go and rest up." Shella hacked a cough, and went back to her room, wheezing and wobbling slightly.

"Oh my Lord," said Cerise, turning to us, "We need to report Charlie to the police for doing that to a minor!"

"It's fine," said Sophia, "Shella will be okay, I'll take good care of her."

"Erm, has Shella's house always been like this?" I asked, looking around at the grimy house.

"You're not the only shocked one," said Bella, "Shella used to have one of the most lovely houses in Parkersburg. Her garden was well-cared for, and absolutely astounding. She had a nice river in the back of her house, but it's just a dried up ditch now for whatever reason. And her house itself, my, my, my. Used to be beautiful inside and outside. God knows what Charlie's done to it."

Ella was already descending into a room below the ground floor. We followed her, and found ourselves in an extensive, circular room with wide walls and low ceilings. Computers and different electronics stood everywhere you looked, and projections of distinct places around the world filled the otherwise blank walls.

"Okay, we each take different computers," I commanded, and everyone rushed to a different computer, "There's plenty for all of us."

I saw Ella enter the computer and check to see if there were any updates on the murder. Sophia printed off the picture of the television screen she had taken, and handed it to Bella who tried matching it to a list of cipher examples she had pulled up on her screen.

Cerise came up to me shyly: "Mind if I work with you, Lex?" she asked.

"Not at all," I said, and pulled up a chair for her, grinning broadly. She sat down, and neatly folded her hands. Sophia printed off several copies of the picture and handed one to us. I dug on the Internet and found a page filled with all the types of ciphers. When you clicked on one cipher name, it took you to a detailed explanation of it.

"Context clues," said Cerise, "They wouldn't just name it randomly. This one has a specific assortment of letters and numbers."

"It's partly split into three divisions," I said, as I scrolled carefully through the hundreds of cipher names.

"Guys, I got it! I matched the picture with this code!" yelled Bella, "It's a trifid cipher!"

"Oh, of course," mumbled Cerise, "Just like you said, Lex. Three divisions like a trifid."

"Yeah," I said, "Great job, Bella. Okay, now we need to decode it." Ella typed something into her computer in a haste, and grabbed a printed copy of the picture. She clicked on a website, and scanned the picture. We all clung onto our chairs in hope something would happen, but a large red "INVALID" flashed across Ella's computer screen. Her face fell in dismay.

"The picture's a bit too blurry, and the computer can't really tell what to decode," explained Ella, "Guess we'll just search up the basic decryption and then convert the encrypted data to its original form ourselves."

Sophia printed off a few trifid cipher code decoders, and the five of us sat there for a few hours, gnawing our pencils and trying to figure it out. The only sound was an occasional mutter or rustle of papers as we wrote and tried to decode the cipher.

I was ever so close to figuring it out as Sophia printed and handed out more trifid cipher code papers. I could tell Cerise had decoded a couple words, and was working on the rest. The trifid cipher combined techniques of fractionation and transposition, which seemed to be going pretty well for me.

"Holy crap," I suddenly said, as I decoded the last layer of the cipher. A cold chill went up my spine, and blackness began to close in on my vision.

"Did you get it?" asked Bella, and everyone huddled around me. I nodded and showed them the paper. Here's what the trifid cipher revealed: This is a message from the Cloaked One. I am coming for everyone in this town who has a connection to the Black Sisterhood. You have been warned...

Everyone around me gasped in shock: "The question is, why?" asked Cerise, and all of us nodded in concurrence. What did the Cloaked One want from us?

CHAPTER TEN

"Well, the Black Sisterhood will have to be shut down," said Sheriff Morber, surrounded by a disarray of papers and letters from people around the town following the attack.

"Please elaborate, sir," said Shella, who had come with us to the Sheriff's station after we had explained to her what was going on.

"What I mean is, no more of this nonsense," said Sheriff Morber, "And not just until the attack stops. I mean forever. Ladies, this organization is a monstrosity and it's completely your fault this has been going on. It's your fault so many people have been murdered. Ever since the beginning."

"Sorry, Sheriff," I said, "But we don't get what you mean by your first response to reading the decryption of the letter. Explain, please."

Sheriff Morber sighed, and threw a cigarette he had been smoking out the window, "You girls can still be friends, but the Black Sisterhood will no longer exist. To be clear, I'm not stopping you from continuing. Frankly, you have permission from

Mayor McFarlin. But, if you wish to cease the attacks, say yes. And the Black Sisterhood will be shut down forever," said Sheriff Morber.

I was fuming on the inside, "No," I blurted out, and everyone turned to me, "Who's to say the attacks will stop? And what're you going to do without us? Don't you dare say you'll be fine, because we decrypted what so many officers and agents couldn't decrypt. The Black Sisterhood will stop at nothing to bring justice to Parkersburg, and stop the Cloaked One once and for all. Who's with me?"

Cerise stepped forward, followed by Sophia and the rest. Sheriff Mother's eyes practically popped out of his head in surprise as he surveyed us.

"Sir, we will not step down from our positions in this town," said Cerise, "It is our job to do what's right, and listening to you isn't."

"Do what you want to, but you'll never take the Black Sisterhood from us," added Shella, "We're here to take down the Cloaked One, and we don't need your help or anyone else's."

"Fine, girls," said Sheriff Morber, slamming his fist on the table, "It's almost as if you want more people to die."

"No, it's almost as if *you* do," said Sophia with narrowed eyes, "Shutting down the Black Sisterhood would be a big mistake on your part, because there's not much you can do without us. Have a good day, Sheriff Clueless."

With that, Sophia flounced out the door and we trailed after her. We walked along the corridors in silence, officers peeking out of their areas to see who had caused such a commotion in the Sheriff's office. Once out in the parking lot, we broke into conversation:

"Without Lex, the Black Sisterhood would already be gone," said Ella, "For sure."

"Agreed," said Sophia, smiling amiably at me, "She saved us down at the Sheriff's office. It was a very brave thing to do, Lex. Very brave to talk to the Sheriff like that."

"You guys talked to him like that, too," I said, blushing a little.

"Oh, stop being modest," said Bella, "We talked because of you. You gave us that determination."

"Well, we can't just lay back now," I said, "I say we investigate the House of Doom. Bring things that'll help us track fingerprints and such. Have I told you guys about the fresh blood?"

Everyone shook their heads, confused. I filled the Black Sisterhood in on how I saw the fresh blood in the House of Doom.

"Well, we'll just have to wait and find out," said Ella.

"Wait?" I asked, outraged at this remark, "C'mon, ladies. Forget the fingerprints. We're collecting blood samples from the fresh blood."

"Good idea," said Cerise, "Where are we going to do the blood analysis?"

"That's not our area of focus right now," I snarled, "We collect some blood samples from around the house, and then figure out where to deliver them to."

"We have to use some kind of tubes to gather the blood and squeeze it into a separate bag," said Shella.

"I have an idea," I said, "We can't mix up the blood, so we have to bring separate cotton swabs and petri dishes. We might discover something from the bacteria growing on the blood, too. We take samples of fresh blood from all around the house, and label the petri dishes. We label them with what floor the blood was on and what room."

"Genius," said Bella, "I know I have cotton swabs and petri dishes at my house. I was doing a project with them in middle school, and bought way too many."

"Bella, your house isn't too far from the House of Doom. Get the stuff, and meet us there in half an hour," I said, and Bella nodded.

"C'mon, guys," said Sophia, "We have to get going." The five of us sprinted off to the House of Doom, our heads clouding with doubt and worry. The run was long, and the pain in my hip began to steadily increase.

When we finally arrived, we were all shaking with fatigue and breathing heavily. Cerise mustered up some strength, pulled herself up from the ground, and walked over to the House of Doom. She kicked the door open, and looked inside.

"Guys?" I asked, sweating profusely even though it was winter, "When you completed Task

Five, did you find anything suspicious in the House of Doom?"

"I was the first one to complete Task Five," said Sophia, "I tested myself to make sure the tasks were reasonable and completable. My mother had the timer, and I completed the task successfully. I didn't find anything suspicious, but it *was* creepy inside the house."

"I was the second to join the Black Sisterhood," said Cerise, "I noticed a faint trace of footsteps underneath the many layers of dust, but didn't think much of it at the time."

I whipped out my phone and typed some notes in, "What about you two?" I asked, addressing Ella and Shella.

"Bella was the third to join, Shella was the fourth, and I was the most recent," said Ella, "Well, that is, *you* were the most recent. When I was completing Task Five, I didn't see anything. But I felt something."

I looked up, puzzled, "Whad' you mean by that?" I questioned, hastily typing notes on my phone.

"I felt as if someone was staring at me the whole time," said Ella, shivering, "When I was by the window, it didn't scare me because I knew that the Black Sisterhood was looking at me. But when I was out of their sight, it was stronger than ever."

"Me too," said Shella, going pale, "It was so frightening." We had all gone eerily quiet, and the only sound was a raven cawing far away. The sky was overcast and gray, and it began to drizzle gently. The bare trees swayed in the frosty wind, and the House of Doom creaked as if stretching its old limbs.

Finally, Bella came running up behind us. She was holding a large wooden crate filled to the brim with cotton swabs and petri dishes, "You ready to go, guys?" she asked, "Why the long faces?"

"Er, nothing," I said, "Everything's alright. Let's get going."

"Lex, where did you notice the fresh blood?" asked Cerise.

"A little bit of everywhere, but mainly the attic on the sixth floor. It was drenched in dried *and* fresh blood," I replied.

Sophia shuddered as we walked through the door Cerise had already kicked open. The house was less scary during the daytime, but still eerie. There wasn't any fresh blood on the first floor, except for the bathroom. Bella took a cotton swab, and swabbed the blood. She put it into the petri dish, and threw the cotton swab on the floor. Ella handed her a permanent marker from the wooden crate Bella had brought, and Bella neatly printed the words: Bathroom, First Floor, House of Doom, on the petri dish.

She handed it to Cerise who dropped it into the wooden crate, "Next floor," said Cerise promptly, and we made our way through the destroyed house and up the stairway.

We ventured through the six, desolate floors of the house, collecting fresh blood samples. By the time our petri dishes were teeming with collected blood and bacteria, and hundreds of cotton balls littered the floor, we were finished.

Bella looked down at the wooden crate filled with no longer empty petri dishes, "Okay, we should locate a lab that does blood testing," she said, "We're bound to get our data in a couple of days."

"Erm, can we please get out of the house first?" asked Shella nervously, "This place is giving me the chills."

"Guys, you can't forget that today is the blood exchange with Lex," said Sophia, as we trooped down the staircase, "As soon as we hand in the blood samples, we have to go to my house and do the blood exchange."

"Chill, Sophia," said Cerise, "We know, but I'm sure Lex and everyone else would agree with me that this is more important at the moment."

"Yeah," I said, "Couldn't have worded it better myself. We'll get to the blood exchange, don't worry about it." Sophia breathed heavily through her nostrils, and we continued our way down the caving in stairs. Cerise kicked open the door again, and I pulled out my phone:

"Guys, there's a lab not too far from here," I announced, "It's a ten-minute walk. The lab is for blood exchange, blood testing, and testing of blood samples. It's called The Lab of Blood."

"Very creative name," said Ella, rolling her eyes sarcastically, "I'm freezing cold, so can we please go inside for a minute before setting off?"

"Sure thing," I said, "We can drink some tea in my house, and then go. Make sure my Mom doesn't see all the blood, she has hemophobia."

"She does? But she always sees blood. On the news, in real life, and so on," said Sophia.

"I'm joking," I said, "She doesn't really have hemophobia, but she'll freak for sure." We sauntered across the lawn leading to my house from the House of Doom. The grass was a dull brown color and crunched softly under my sneakers. An owl hooted bleakly from the tree branches, and the House of Doom loomed over us with some kind of a towering fate.

The door was locked and all the curtains were closed. When Cerise rang the doorbell, Mom thrust the door open. There were massive bags under her eyes, and she was holding a kitchen knife. Her tense face relaxed when she saw us, and she put down the knife.

"Er, Mom, what were you doing with a knife?" I asked.

"Never know who'll be ringing at your door these days," said Mom, giving me a large hug, "Never mind me, how are you girls?"

"Fine," replied Ella, "Lex offered to warm up a bit in your house, Mrs. Torres. We then have to go somewhere."

Mom welcomed us in graciously, "I have a guest, but he'll be leaving soon," she said. My jaw dropped open when I walked into the kitchen and found Albert holding a cup of tea and wearing Dad's bathrobe.

"Um, Lex?" said Sophia, "Are you just as surprised as I am?" I threw a quick glance at Cerise, who nodded, indicating for me to tell the truth.

"No, not really," I answered, trying not to make eye contact with Sophia, "The first time it happened I didn't even tell *Mom*. I'd never experienced anything like it before."

Sophia wore an ashen face as she looked from me to Albert, "Wait," she began, lost for words, "So... this has been going on for a while now?"

"Kinda, I guess," I said in response, and Sophia laughed. She shook her head and sat down.

"Being best friends with you is like exploring a labyrinth that's constantly changing," said Sophia, "I hate it, but I love it at the same time."

"Are you mad?" I asked tentatively. Sophia laughed again and shook her head "no". She poured herself a cup of tea and began drinking. Everyone else followed her lead and swarmed around the tea kettle, desperate to warm up.

I drank some green tea and immediately felt warmth spread through my body. The green tea fell down my throat and enveloped my body in a strange tranquility.

After the Black Sisterhood and I had regained most of our strength, we thanked Mom and went outside. We walked to The Lab of Blood in silence and sat in the lobby area, waiting to be called forward by a doctor who could assist us.

"Hey," whispered Cerise in my ear. Her voice made my heart freeze and all my worries go away, "Why do you think Albert was dressed in your Dad's bathrobe?"

That's exactly when I realized just how clueless I was about everything. I turned to Cerise and shrugged, frowning.

"Are you here for a blood analysis?" asked a sharp voice behind me, bringing me back to reality.

All my worries crashed back into me like a tidal wave, submerging me in despair.

"Uh, no, actually," responded Bella, "We have blood samples that we found in the House of Doom." I gave Bella a strong kick and she yelped quietly.

"Sorry," I said, "The girl's slightly bonkers, doesn't know what she's saying. We're doing blood analysis for a school science project."

"Dangerous times to be wandering around the streets," said the doctor skeptically, "I'll get you with a doctor that will do a DNA analysis of the blood shortly."

"Thanks," I said and curtly smiled at Bella who was shaking with laughter.

"Now I have to pretend like I'm a lunatic!" cried Bella, gasping for air, "Thanks a bunch, Lex!" She wiggled her fingers by her ears and stuck out her tongue, swiveling her eyes around.

I rolled my eyes, but couldn't help smiling. A man with a long brown beard and glasses came up to the six of us, and we all quit laughing.

"Follow me, sisters," whispered the man.

We all exchanged strange looks. Had we just heard the man call us "sisters"? Sophia tentatively stepped into the room, followed by Cerise and everybody else. I was the last to come in, and the doctor pulled the door shut behind me. He clicked the lock into place.

"Hello!" cried the man loudly, startling us all, "Sophia, oh God. *I* was one of the greatest friends of your father! I know *all* about the Black Sisterhood."

Sophia's mouth dropped open and she gave the man a hug, "Hildred!" she squealed, "You would come to our house back when I was a kid. You would always bring me boxes and boxes filled with my favorite candies! How did I not recognize you? Why do you no longer visit us?"

"Your father and I got into an argument, I'm afraid," said Hildred, sighing sadly, "Said I was giving you too many sweets, and that you would throw temper tantrums because of how sugar high you were. After that, we stopped talking altogether. All connection broke off between the two of us. None remained."

Sophia looked disheartened, "I'm ever so sorry to hear that!" she said, "Anyways, we're here for a DNA analysis of some blood samples."

"Did you get them on the street?" asked Hildred, raising a suspicious eyebrow. Sophia nodded to us, motioning that he was somebody we could trust.

"No, Hildred, I'm afraid not," said Sophia, "I wish the blood was that innocent. House of Doom. Fresh blood in the House of Doom, believe it or not."

Hildred gasped, nearly dropping the pair of gloves he was putting on, "My, my!" he moaned, clutching his face, "Top priority."

"Please don't tell any of the doctors!" I begged, and Hildred grinned. He closed his mouth and pretended to zip it shut.

"Who are you?" asked Hildred, gently taking the blood samples, "Friend or foe?"

"Friend by far," said Sophia, and put an arm around my shoulder, "New member!"

"That's great, congrats!" cried Hildred, as he began doing something with the blood samples,

"Did your suspicion arouse during Task Five, Miss Whoever You May Be?"

"I'm Alexis Torres," I said, "But you can call me Lexie. And, yes, my suspicion did indeed arouse during Task Five."

After exchanging some small talk with Hildred, he began talking to everybody else. I sat in the corner, massaging my shoulders and thinking about who the blood could possibly belong to. Cerise sat by me, and I squeezed her hand gently.

"Polished and sent in!" cried Hildred, turning back around, "A letter will be emailed to you in the mail tomorrow morning. It will contain the DNA results of every single blood sample. Have a nice day, my friends! Hope to see you again sometime soon."

"Bye, Hildred," muttered Sophia, and gave him a friendly kiss on the cheek. We all filed out, obviously worried about the results that would come in the mail tomorrow morning.

Tomorrow morning would prove to be a catastrophe of all sorts. I could already tell without any results or any fortune tellers. Something about the blood samples just didn't seem right...

CHAPTER ELEVEN

I woke up the next morning to someone frantically ringing the doorbell. All thoughts of school gone, I scrambled out of bed. Mom and Carly were down in the kitchen, frying eggs and making pancakes. Carly still looked extremely ill and she smiled weakly at me as I passed. I couldn't help but notice all of the medicine bottles on the counter. "Good morning, honey!" said Mom, "Sophia and the Black Sisterhood are practically busting the door down. I suggest you go and check on them. "

"Does Carly have to take that much medicine? " I blurted out, my eyes stinging with tears. Mom 's face fell and she followed my gaze to the medicine bottles on the counter.

"She's a little sick," admitted Mom, "Her body is still recovering, but I swear to you that everything will be okay. The doctor said she's expected to recover in a few weeks."

Carly smiled at me again, and I gave her a long hug. I drew back, tears filling my eyes. Not wanting to upset her, I turned away and quickly wiped them with my sleeve.

"I'm going to go open the door, " I rasped, and panic immediately surged through my body. Had the DNA analysis results come in? Sophia 's face was squashed against the door frame, looking terrified.

I quickly unlocked the door and opened it. Bella, Ella, Shella, and Cerise were standing behind Sophia. They all looked terror-stricken beyond belief.

"I was about to bust down the door, " said Sophia gutturally, "We have to talk right now. " I noticed she was holding several stacks of papers, more than just the results.

Mom and Carly barely noticed their entrance. They were laughing and eating at the breakfast table, as if nothing was wrong. As if Sophia hadn't just entered holding papers of doom.

Sophia sniffled, barely holding back tears. Unable to control herself and tell me something, she threw the papers at me. Everyone else held their breaths, waiting for my reaction. I scanned all the results and dropped the papers in horror.

"Yes! " cried Sophia, still snuffling, "That is the blood of Roberto and Olga, Archer 's family, your father, and so on. And look underneath! "

My heart pounding, I threw the results on the floor and pulled a freshly printed newspaper out from underneath. My heart stopped and I felt as if I was thousands of feet underwater. The article read:

HILDRED DARROLDS STABBED IN APARTMENT; CLOAKED ONE OR NOT?

Hildred Darrolds, worker at the Lab of Blood, was found murdered in his apartment late yesterday night. Hildred is still alive and receiving treatment at iHealthy Hospital. Police strongly encourage everyone to lock their doors and enforce stricter protection measures on their homes.

"The Cloaked One is killing off everyone with a connection to the Black Sisterhood, " I said, a lump forming in my throat, "We don't know why, but we do know that that's the truth. And Hildred had a connection to your father who has a connection to you. "

"I wonder why the Cloaked One didn 't fully kill him, " said Shella thoughtfully, "I mean, surely it wasn't an accident, right? "

"We have to pay Hildred a visit," I said firmly, "We know where he is. They said it was iHealthy Hospital. Let 's go there right now, eh? "

"You haven 't seen all of the papers yet, " said Sophia hoarsely, "The Cloaked One left us a message. "

I felt my whole body go numb as I lay the newspaper aside. A bunch of graph papers with criss crossed lines on them sat in a neat stack. A sticky note that had CO scrawled on it was on top of the papers.

"Some kind of puzzle, " said Sophia, hands shaking, "But there 's no rules. If you look closely, there 's a specific pattern going down the right side of each graph and set of criss crossed lines. We have to arrange it in perfect order, so each pattern matches up. Then we'll be able to decode something. "

"Smart thinking, " I said, barely able to swallow, "We have to split up. The decoding will take a long time, so we need four people to stay here and work on it. Two others go to iHealthy. "

"You and Cerise can go, " said Ella, "The rest of us will stay and decode. Ask him about what happened. See how he is. "

"Sure, " said Cerise, and clasped my hand, "We'll drive there, I 'm tired of walking. "

"Works for me, " I replied. Before following Cerise out the door, I turned back to the kitchen. Carly was chugging down a cup of medicine, grimacing as she swallowed it. Mom patted her head and rinsed the cup with water as Carly sat back down.

Emotional pain consumed me and tears slipped from my eyes. My cheeks were burning with wetness and I averted my eyes from the sight that brought me so much regret and nostalgia for when things were okay.

I looked down to find Shella, Sophia, Bella, and Ella busy at work. They were decoding the words, lining up the patterns, and silently marking things down on paper. Cerise called my name from outside, and I walked out the door.

She kissed my cheek as I sat in the car, and I felt my head collapse into her lap. Cerise started up the car and drove to iHealthy, occasionally stroking my hair. Thoughts and possibilities filled my head as we drove soundlessly to the hospital where Hildred resided.

Encapsulated by my train of ideas, I barely noticed as Cerise parked the car and got out. My head fell to the car seat and I sluggishly dragged myself out behind Cerise.

"You okay? " asked Cerise, and I nodded. We proceeded in quietude and I collapsed into a seat as Cerise strode up to a doctor. Cerise talked to the doctor for quite a long time, but I hardly discerned what was going on.

I felt dizzy and light headed as Cerise gesticulated for me to come over. My head felt like a vast ocean with so many questions swimming inside of it, waiting to be answered. But I knew that answers would lead to more questions, and the pressure would make me explode.

"Er, Lex? " whispered Cerise, "The doctor 's taking us to Hildred. I told her we were his nieces and she agreed, not really questioning it. You sure you 're okay? "

"I 'm fine, " I mumbled, staring down at my feet. My neck ached, but I refused to look up. I felt too dizzy.

"If you say so, " said Cerise, sounding a little dejected. We entered a white room with colorful tiles on the floor. The room had flickering lights and smelled like a typical hospital. A bed where Hildred lay stood in the center, and a couple wires were attached to him. Machines that recorded his heart rate, body temperature, and so on stood around Hildred. His eyes were closed and he was muttering something underneath his breath.

"You have fifteen minutes on the clock, " the doctor said tersely, and shut the door behind us. Cerise nudged me forward and I anxiously approached Hildred. His eyes shot open, making me jump five feet in the air.

"Jeez, Hildred, " I chuckled, "You scared me there. " I stopped when I noticed how pale he was. His eyes looked like pallid white and bloodshot orbs reflecting in an eerie yellow light.

"Alexis, "murmured Hildred, not sounding like himself, "Cerise. How do you do? " His head snapped in the direction of Cerise, and he smiled in a sinister way.

"Hey, Hildred, " I said, backing up a couple steps, "Sorry about what happened last night. "

Hildred 's eyes rolled into the back of his head, and he began thrashing uncontrollably in the bed. I considered screaming for the doctor, when he suddenly stopped. His eyes were back to normal and he spoke in a hurried tone.

"Cerise, Lexie, nice to see you guys! " said Hildred, "Listen you have to help me. The Cloaked One has got me under control- " Hildred stopped and his eyes rolled back into his head again. He thrashed even more, and his uncanny robotic state was back.

"Alexis, " he said, "Cerise. How do you do? " His head snapped in my direction, and he cackled. His hand came up to his throat and he began choking himself.

"Hildred, stop! " I screeched.

"This is fun, " said Hildred in his monotone voice, "Maybe the Cloaked One should 've finished me off after all. I like pain. "

"Hildred, you don 't know what you 're talking about! " squealed Cerise. Hildred went back into his eyes-rolling-back-thrashing-around state and returned to normal.

"Please, " he said, breathing heavily, "When the Cloaked One doesn't have me under control, I can't say a spare word. You have to help me. Tell Sophia immediately. The Cloaked One didn 't kill me because I broke off connections with Sophia 's father. He injured me, but planted something in my brain that allows him to control me at free will."

"Hildred! " I cried, tears flowing down my cheeks, "Do the doctors know? "
"No, they just think I 'm absolutely nuts, " replied Hildred, "I don't know what to do. The Cloaked One broke into my house late at night while I was making myself a midnight snack. He grabbed me by the collar and stabbed me in the stomach. My apartment is up on the third floor, so the Cloaked One fled through the window. "

"Hildred! " said Cerise, "We'll get you help. We'll get you out of here. We'll tell the doctors the truth. "

Hildred snapped back into his creepy state, "No, you won't! " he snarled in an inhumane voice, and leapt from his bed. He sprinted across the room and grabbed Cerise by the shirt.

I watched, frozen, as Hildred threw her into the wall with some kind of sadistic strength. Her head hit the wall and a sickening crunch filled the room. I ran over and smacked Hildred in the face. He collapsed to the floor, writhing uncontrollably, and returned to his ordinary state.

"Cerise! " cried Hildred, as Cerise emerged from the ground, moaning, "God, I'm so sorry! I'm turning into a maniac! Please help me! Please!"

"We'll help you, Hildred, " I scowled, helping Cerise up, "Is there any way you can fight the pressure off? "

"I've tried, trust me! " said Hildred, eyes bulging, "You guys never should have come to visit me. I'm turning absolutely crazy! What else do you want from me before I lash out like this again? "

"I think we should let you rest, " said Cerise coldly, but her eyes softened when she saw Hildred squirming on the floor in pain. We dragged him back into bed. Luckily for us, he was still connected to the wires.

Hildred took a deep breath and rested his hands on his stomach. I noticed that they were all up scratched up. Taking advantage of the fact that Hildred was back to normal, I asked:

"Does the Cloaked One make you hurt yourself?" Hildred looked up with wide, teary eyes and nodded.

Cerise sobbed into her hands, patting Hildred 's hand. Just as he opened his mouth to say something, his eyes became bloodshot and his hands rose to his throat.

Cerise quickly removed her hand as if she had touched a hot surface, and we sprung off of the bed Hildred was lying in. He began floundering in bed, choking himself, veins throbbing in his neck.

His head began pulsating strangely, and his legs twisted around. He screamed in an unearthly way, and Cerise and I dashed to get a doctor. Several doctors rushed in and restrained Hildred, pulling his hands and legs down.

"Go now! " yelled a doctor, pointing at the door. Cerise and I hurtled out and scrambled into the car.

We were too stunned to talk, and had to catch our breath for a moment in the car. My body couldn't keep up with my racing mind, and I threw myself down at the seat in exasperation.

"We. Have. To. Get. To. Sophia. Now!" pronounced Cerise, and started up the car without buckling up. She zoomed back to my house, going way beyond the speed limit. When we had arrived, the car skidded to a stop with an ear splitting s*creech!* and Cerise yanked the door open.

We dashed into the house, not closing the car doors behind us. The rest of the Black Sisterhood was anxiously sitting on the couch when we bolted in. Sophia jumped to her feet and steadied Cerise as she nearly collided with Bella.

"The Cloaked One. Is. Controlling. Hildred, " panted Cerise, and passed out on the floor. I felt as if I was underwater, and the voices around me were miles away, echoing vaguely. Mom rushed out to help Cerise, and everyone else crowded around me.

"Leave Lex alone, " said Sophia firmly, and pressed a cup of cold water to my lips. I drank gratefully, pausing for gasps of breath.

"What happened? " asked Carly, who had entered the room, "Is she okay?"

Carly indicated Cerise, and Sophia nodded.

"She'll be fine, " said Sophia, "Lex, can you tell us what happened, please?" I filled Sophia, Bella, Ella, Shella, and Carly in on what had happened at iHealthy.

Shella looked unusually green. She keeled over and vomited all over the rug, Bella following her. Ella simply sobbed into her hands. To us, it seemed as if the problem couldn't get any worse.

"Did you figure out the code?" I asked, still trembling. Sophia moisted my forehead with a wet towel.

"No," said Sophia, "We wanted to wait for you guys." She looked over, and I followed her gaze to Cerise who was lying on the floor. Cerise groaned as Mom helped her up.

"Did you figure out any words? " I asked, feeling a slight frustration.

"Yeah, " grumbled Sophia moodily, "We got the words I and Raems. I think we have to unscramble or something, 'cause it doesn't make much sense. "

"We'll figure it out once we crack all the words," I snapped, "Let Cerise rest, she's had quite the morning. Being thrown into a wall and terrorized."

"So have you, " murmured Sophia, "You should go rest, too. "

"No, " I protested, "I want to stay with you guys. I'll be fine. Hildred attacked Cerise. She's in pain. You guys should've heard the crunch when she hit the wall. Scared me half to death. "

"You look a little off, " said Shella, wiping vomit from the corners of her mouth, "Are you alright? "

"Be quiet, Shella, " snarled Sophia, "She's not alright, and neither is Cerise. Can we just continue decoding? "

"Smartest thing I've heard you say all day," I chuckled, and Sophia elbowed me playfully.

"We've figured out two words, " said Bella, "But we have to unscramble, I think. "

"Sophia already told me, " I responded, kneeling down by all the papers and grids, "Let 's get to work. Where'd you guys stop? "

Ella indicated the papers, "The ones that are crossed off are the ones we 've done, " she said, "We have to start a new word, so don 't look for a specific pattern. "

I rummaged through all the papers and the Black Sisterhood knelt by me. We began connecting the lines that corresponded, finding patterns. It was much harder and much more confusing than I had expected, but we had gotten a couple more words in a few hours.

"I, Raems, Hserf, Doolb, Fo, Wen, Smitciv, " said Sophia, emphasizing my confusion, "Everything 's crossed off. We 're done. "

"Done?! " I exclaimed, throwing myself to the ground, "This makes no sense whatsoever! "

"I can help, " a weak voice muttered behind us. I whipped around to find Carly standing by the couch.

"Carly, " I said, exasperated, "Sorry, but we don't need you right now. You can go. " Carly recoiled as the sharp rebukes came spilling out of my mouth.

"Wow, " she whispered, "Okay. I'm here if you need me. "

I felt guilt sting my insides, "Okay, listen!" I called after her, "I didn't mean any of that. Sorry. You can come help us if you want. "

A smile showed on Carly's face like a bright beacon, and she hugged me, "I have an idea, " she said, "Why don't Sophia and Lex go check on Cerise? She's not feeling well. The rest of us can work on the words."

I nodded and turned to Sophia, "Yes, " I said, and narrowed my eyebrows at Sophia's condescending expression, "Cerise got thrown into a wall. Her head was bleeding like crazy. She needs some company. "

"Fine, " said Sophia, her voice laced with a hint of annoyance, "Let's go."

Carly joined Bella, Ella, and Shella on the floor. They began to write down possible solutions for all the words, while Sophia and I climbed up the flight of steps leading to the guest bedroom where Cerise was.

Mom was in the room, delicately feeding Cerise spoonfuls of porridge. She turned around when she heard us enter the room. I noticed how awfully tired she looked.

"We'll take it from here, Mom, " I said, kissing Mom on the cheek.

"Thanks, girls, " said Mom, "I'm going to go start preparing dinner." Mom walked out of the room, and Sophia closed the door.

I gingerly walked up to Cerise but Sophia stayed behind. I noticed a scowl plastered on her face and the way she crossed her arms. Cerise groaned as I stroked her hair.

"That hurts, " she moaned, pulling the covers over her face, "That hurts, Mrs. Torres. "

"It's me, Lexie, " I said gently, and Cerise shot up from the covers. She grabbed my hand and leaned in to hug me.

"Lex! " cried Cerise, "Thank you so much for coming. Your Mom's been doing such a great job of taking care of me, I can't thank her enough! "

"Calm down, " I said, and eased Cerise back into bed, "How are you? "

"Still hurts like hell, " answered Cerise, "Don't feel too good, either. How are the words coming along?"

"I, Raems, Hserf, Doolb, Fo, Wen, Smitciv," I said in response, and a look of confusion passed over Cerise's face, "Those are the words. Carly, Bella, Shella, and Ella are working on unscrambling them."

"Oh, " said Cerise, "By the way, a doctor's coming to visit tomorrow. Your Mom told him I fell off a bike and injured my head really badly. He scolded your Mom for not reminding me to put a helmet on. I have to pretend as if I'm her daughter now. Where's Sophia? "

Sophia emerged from the shadows and scowled at Cerise, "Hello," she said coldly, "How are you feeling? "

"What's wrong? " I asked defensively as Cerise cowered under her blanket, "What did Cerise do? "

"She walked in, said something incoherent, and passed out on the floor, " said Sophia, "She 's losing strength, I tell you. Physical and mental."

I sprung up from the bed, grabbed Sophia by the collar, and raised her up, "Hildred slammed her into a wall, " I said through gritted teeth, "Can't you tell she feels like trash? "

"She didn 't fight him off, " said Sophia, not in the least bit scared.

"I did, " I said, "I smacked him to get him back into his ordinary state, while Cerise was recovering. She didn't pass out when she was thrown into the wall. Some kind of weakness that is, huh?"

"I don 't even know what I'm saying, " said Sophia, "I have no right to do this. Cerise, I'm really sorry. I've just been so high-strung lately. It's crazy. "

"Doesn't give you an excuse for getting mad at someone who nearly got killed, " I grumbled, "But it's fine, whatever. You can go down, I'll feed Cerise."

"Okay, " murmured Sophia and turned to leave. When she had closed the door behind her, I sat back down. Cerise was asleep. I pressed my lips to her forehead, and drew back, startled. A raging fever had started up in her and her whole body was hot.

I moistened her forehead and dry lips, and slipped medicine through her open mouth. Once her body had cooled down a bit, I headed downstairs.

"Cerise is sick, " I said, not noticing the long faces surrounding me, "I gave her some medicine."

"Sit down," said Carly gravely. Confused, I took a seat on the couch and surveyed everyone.

"Guys, what 's wrong?" I asked, "Did you figure out the message? "

"I Smear Fresh Blood Of New Victims, " said Shella, her voice quivering, "That's what the message said."

CHAPTER TWELVE

I stood, stunned and speechless. My blood froze in my veins. The world seemed to have stopped, and I could hear my heart thumping loudly.

"You're telling me," I began, not quite sure what to say, "That the Cloaked One keeps his victims' blood and smears it around the House of Doom?"

Everyone nodded, and I felt sick to my stomach. I looked around, and caught Ella's eye. She had some kind of determination shining on her face that puzzled me.

"This is madness!" I cried, slamming my fist onto the table, "This has to be stopped. Someone, come with me to the House of Doom."

"No, Lex, you can't-" began Sophia, grabbing my arm.

"Now!" I roared, spit flying from my mouth, yanking my arm away from Sophia, "Sheriff Morber is *wrong*. This isn't our fault, but it's still happening. More people are going to die if we sit around and whine. We have to go to the House of Doom and stay there overnight to see if anything happens. Everyone else, you can go home. Who's coming?"

"Me," said Ella in a steely tone, "I'll come with you, Lex." A tense silence passed between everybody. Sophia finally stood up, breaking it.

"C'mon, Shella," she said, "You can come home with me because of Charlie. Let Lex and Ella be fools. There's nothing we can do to stop them."

"Let's not go tonight, though," said Ella, and I glared at her. She backed away to join Sophia, Bella, and Shella. Carly sat on the couch, still as a statue.

"Fine," I grumbled, and Sophia glowered at me, "Fine, Ella, fine. I'm going alone."

"You can't," blurted out Carly, "It's way too dangerous. Better you wait and go with Ella. That'll be safer."

"Jeez!" I exclaimed and threw my hands into the air, "When are we going, Ella?"

"Give it a week," said Sophia, "I won't come with you guys, but if you really insist it, fine. But I suggest you give it a week. So next Tuesday. Let's go, Shella."

Shella and Sophia turned around and walked away, heads bent. Bella shrugged and waved goodbye before following them out. Ella tilted her head like a curious puppy.

"Well, I'll see you soon," she said and smiled promptly, "Sorry it had to be delayed."

"Forget it," I said curtly, "We're going next Tuesday, anyway. Leave." Ella puffed out some air and walked out, slamming the door behind her.

I sighed and sat down, rubbing my temples. I turned to Mom who was holding a tray filled with plates of lasagna. She looked confused.

"They left," I said, and leaned over to kiss Mom on the cheek, "I'm going to bed early. I'm sleeping in the guest bedroom today. With Cerise."

I collapsed into bed by Cerise who was fast asleep. She looked so peaceful, so innocent, lying there in bed, hands crossed over her stomach. Tears filled my eyes and I cried myself to sleep. Nothing in the world was right. Except for Cerise. She made things seem like they were going to be okay. Even if I knew they weren't.

I woke to morning light seeping in through the curtains of the guest bedroom. The bed next to me was still occupied by Cerise, who seemed sicker than ever.

"Mom!" I croaked, still half asleep, "When's the doctor coming?"

"He's here," said Mom, and I realized with alarm that it was already ten thirty in the morning, "Can you please wake Cerise up, dear?"

I shook Cerise and she woke up, coughing and groaning. She smiled when she saw me, but was too weak to make any words come out.

"The doctor's here," I uttered, "You'll be better soon." She pressed her cold palm against my cheek and I felt a tear trickling down it. It slid into the folds of her hand and she smiled again.

"Thank you," whispered Cerise, "Tell your Mom the doctor can come in." I called for Mom, slowly rising from bed. She and a doctor came into the room. The doctor didn't even acknowledge me as he walked up to Cerise and surveyed her with a thoughtful countenance.

"Ask her to leave," the doctor said shortly, nodding towards me. I whispered "It's going to be okay" to Cerise before turning around and making my way downstairs.

My jaw dropped to the floor when I saw who was sitting there. It was Sophia and her face was covered in tears. She ran up to me and squeezed me into a tight hug.

"Lex!" she cried, "I've had the worst morning and night ever!"

"What's wrong?" I asked, "Did anyone else get killed?"

Sophia nodded so quickly, I thought her head would snap off, "Dillon!" she sobbed, mascara running down her face, "Albert, too!"

I felt bile surging up my throat, "What?" I asked, "When?"

"This morning!" she said, thrusting a newspaper into my hands. I scanned the cover which had a picture of Albert and Dillon standing together by a motorcycle shop.

"The police found them dead in their house at three in the morning," I read from the newspaper, "Their neighbor heard screaming and called the police. She said she saw a cloaked figure escaping the house and running into the woods." I looked up in terror. Sophia was rocking back and forth, wailing like a banshee.

"Who else knows?" I asked, "Why didn't the neighbor run after the Cloaked One?"

"She's not an idiot, Lex!" screeched Sophia, "He was *armed*! It seems to me as if the Cloaked One is killing off everyone who is especially close to the Black Sisterhood. Except for Roberto and Olga who he was partly using."

"Yeah," I replied, pacing the room, "The Cloaked One was meeting Roberto and Olga somewhere and forcing them to do that horrible stuff. And then he killed them with the chips."

"I texted everyone else, but I thought I'd tell you in person," said Sophia, "And also, I thought you'd be the first I'd tell about a letter I got from the Cloaked One. Before I show you, how's Cerise?"

"Still really sick," I said, curiosity eating me alive, "The doctor's seeing her right now, and he'll prescribe some medication. Can I see the letter now?"

"Sure," mumbled Sophia, handing me a letter, "This one isn't too bad though."

The letter was made of letters cut from newspapers to disguise the Cloaked One's handwriting. It said: *I may be the Cloaked One, but I have a helper. I have a helper who kills for me. They do this against their will, for I keep them going through threats. I, the Cloaked One, met with Roberto and Olga. I am the one devising all the wonderful plans. But I have a helper. A helper who kills for me.*

I was stunned, horrified, absolutely thunderstruck. The Cloaked One had a helper. It wasn't really the Cloaked One killing, it was his helper. His helper who he was forcing to kill.

"Figuring this whole thing out is like playing a game of "cat and mouse" with the Cloaked One," I said, "He keeps on dangling something before us, then pulls it away and we're left completely clueless. Now that I think of it, I've kept a very important piece of information from you guys. I've seen the Cloaked One with a different person before, but didn't think about it. I always thought the Cloaked One acted alone."

"Me too," said Sophia, "But now we know the truth. We have to give this letter to the police."

"Bad idea," I said, "They'll tell us to stop investigating and intercept everything that comes our way. Best we figure something out ourselves."

Sophia hesitated for a moment, but then nodded unyieldingly, "You're right," she said, "You and Ella can go to the House of Doom next Tuesday and stay there overnight. Kudos to you two for being so brave. Especially you, Lex. We wouldn't have gotten anywhere without you in the Black Sisterhood."

"We have to find out more about Dillon's and Albert's murder," I said, grabbing the newspaper, "It says here that the police and SWAT team are doing a detailed investigation of the house this afternoon. We have to go with them."

"You're mad!" exclaimed Sophia, "They'd throw our butts into jail if we even proposed the idea. We'll go later when they leave."

"Sophia," I said, "We have to go to the police station. Without the police knowing. I feel like there's more to this than they're saying in the newspaper."

"Yeah, no shit," said Sophia, "The police of Parkersburg have a reputation of lying to the citizens of Parkersburg. Let's go."

"Can you call Bella, Ella, and Shella to stay with Cerise?" I asked, anxiety pulsating through my body, "I don't want her to stay alone. Tell them about what we're doing and also tell them to tell Cerise."

"We're crazy to be doing this," muttered Sophia, "But awfully brave. We'll sneak in and take it from there. Your Mom and Carly can keep Cerise company. Bella, Ella, and Shella are occupied today."

"How?" I asked, tightening my laces.

"Er, they're having a girls' day at the spa," said Sophia, rolling her eyes, "I was too upset to come, and knew you and Cerise would turn the generous offer down."

"Generous," I said, "Pfft." Sophia opened the door and I walked out into the air laced with approaching spring. My blood burned as I watched a police car with turned on sirens race in the direction of Daniel's house. Something didn't seem right.

Sophia scrambled into the driver's seat and I buckled up in the passenger's seat. She drove off and parked a little ways away from the police station, concealing the car behind a bush.

I slipped the kitchen knife into the pocket of my black sweater, and Sophia hid the gun in her already hunky boots. We got down on hands and knees like wild animals and clambered towards the police station. We dove behind a tree as an officer walked by, armed with a massive AK-47.

Once he had passed, we continued our way towards the police station. Once inside, everything became much more difficult. Police officers swarmed around everywhere, armed with guns and all sorts of weapons.

Sophia and I crouched low to the ground, continuously having to dive behind desks and shelves of guns. We had to clamber through the kitchen in the police station, and Sophia crashed into a stack of pots lying in the corner on the floor.

"Who puts pots on the floor?" questioned Sophia, looking disgusted while I shushed her with panic.

We stopped by the bathroom to stretch our legs and luckily encountered nobody. As we were walking out, a woman in uniform walked in. Sophia and I rushed to the nearest stall, locked the door, and stood up on the toilet. We held our breaths, and I slipped my foot into the toilet by accident.

The dirty water penetrated me and I gasped silently. Sophia put a hand over my mouth, cautiously unlocked the door, and we ran out of the restrooms.

We ascended two flights of stairs, blending in due to our black clothes. Sophia pulled out her gun at one point to seem more realistic. I coaxed her into putting it away as we attracted strange glances from passing police officers. Luckily, not one of them asked for our ID.

"Sheriff Morber came to visit today," we heard a police officer say to his buddy, "It's about tha' secret Daniel thing they won't tell any of the citizens about. Most of the officers don' even know what they're doing."

"I reckon they'll tell everyone soon enough," his buddy answered, "Sheriff Morber's talkin' to Officer Wilkins righ' now, eh? Never knew Officer Wilkins would play such an important role."

They both guffawed rather stupidly and continued their descent down the stairs. Sophia and I exchanged an excited glance, and I whispered a plan into Sophia's ear. She nodded, and removed her gun from her pocket.

"Let's go get "em," I muttered into Sophia's ear, and we wandered around the station, nobody paying much attention to us.

We found the two cleaning ladies in the kitchen, sweeping up the floors. Sophia calmly strode up to them, and I took out my knife.

"An officer threw up in a room upstairs," said Sophia, "We'll show you to it."

"Carla, you stay here," said one cleaning lady with a thick accent, "I go."

"No, we need all hands on deck," I said, "Erm, Carla should come, too."

"Bah!" yelled the cleaning lady christened Carla and gathered all her cleaning supplies, "You no important, Natalia." The cleaning lady, Natalia, smacked Carla across the face with her rag.

"Follow us, ladies," I said, trying to ignore their humorous behavior, "To the elevator if you please. Gotta have an empty one to fit all your supplies."

Sophia pressed a few buttons and we waited for an empty elevator, "Ah, there we go," she murmured, and we all clambered in. Once the doors had closed, Sophia and I acted immediately.

I struck Natalia across the head and body slammed her in the elevator. She tried to kick me in the leg, but I caught it and twisted it back. Natalia grunted in pain, but wasn't giving up.

She grabbed my arm and yanked it down. I lost my balance, tripped, and fell on top of her. Using this as an advantage, she tried to get up, but I pinned her down to the ground.

"You no officer!" struggled Natalia, before passing out. I grabbed her cleaning cart and tore her apron and name tag off of her, sticking it onto myself.

I heard Sophia trying to hold back Carla, but she was a tougher one. Carla lunged on me from the back, knocking me onto the floor. I sprung up and swung my leg up from behind, hitting her square in the face.

She collided with the wall with a light "uh!" and Sophia shoved on Carla's apron and name tag, grabbing her cleaning cart. Wiping the sweat from my face, I grabbed a broom and jammed it into the elevator doors as we walked out.

"I'm going to put a Caution sign up for now," I said, and produced one from the cart, "No one'll come near the elevator for the time being."

"Good job, Natalia," said Sophia, high fiving me with a wink.

"Likewise, Carla," I said back, and we snickered together. An officer passing by smiled and waved at us with a friendly gesture.

"Hello!" he said, casually whistling, "Jammed elevator? I'll tell all the officers not to use it for now."

"Thank you!" I called, attempting Natalia's accent, "No good when jammed. Caution sign put up."

"Right!" called the officer, saluting us. He disappeared behind a set of glass doors and Sophia and I set off to find Officer Wilkins' office.

"Here!" suddenly said Sophia in a strained whisper, and I whipped around to find that she was right. A name tag that said in neat letters Officer Jonathan Wilkins was plastered near a door that led into a very wide and spacious office.

"I'll collect the trash, you sweep the floor," said Sophia, "Get as much information as possible. We have to know what they're up to. We have to know if they're in some kind of danger. And remember, heads bent, eyes down."

I nodded, my heart drumming loudly against my ribcage. Sophia opened the door and walked in, humming a tune. She picked up the trash can and began emptying it into her cart, taking as much time as possible.

I followed lead and walked into the room. Out of the corner of my eye, I saw Sheriff Morber and a plump, red faced man sitting at a desk.

"Let me repeat the plan, Jonathan," Sheriff Morber said in a strict tone, "Don't worry about the old cleaning hags, they won't understand nuthin'."

Anger boiled in my veins, but I continued sweeping, acting as clueless and innocent as possible. I could see Sophia purposely drop some trash and pretend to pick it up, just to extend her time.

"A SWAT team *will* be investigating Daniel's house, but that's not our area of focus," said Sheriff Morber, "We will use sirens and everything else as bait to lure out the Cloaked One. He will come at night. Following his recent patterns, we are almost certain he will show up there tonight."

"Yes sir," said Officer Wilkins, "Please continue."

"When he appears, a few officers will follow behind him in a regular dusty forest cart some villager boys use to play," said Sheriff Morber, "We'll catch him once and for all. We'll all be armed and stocked with supplies."

"You'll be wearing your uniforms?" asked Officer Wilkins, a line of sweat clearly visible on his upper lip, "Or some kind of a disguise?"

"We'll be wearing plain old clothes boys these days would wear," responded Sheriff Morber, "All of our weapons will be in satchels we've seen them use to store toys."

"If I may ask, where is the cart that you will be using located?" asked Officer Wilkins, leaning in. Sheriff Morber simply backed away, dramatically rolling his eyes.

"Police shed along with all the cars," he answered stiffly, throwing me a look of suspicion, "I won't be accompanying the officers. I'll be working in my office."

I gathered Natalia's cleaning supplies and wandered out, still trying to act oblivious. I nudged Sophia on the way out, and she caught on. We walked out and back to the "jammed" elevator.

"My God," said Sophia, collapsing against the cool wall of the elevator. I unjammed the broomstick and shoved the Caution sign back into my cart.

"Why would they do something so barbaric?" I asked, as we changed back into our clothes and shook Natalia and Carla awake.

"What happening?" asked Natalia, a massive bruise forming on her forehead.

"I don't know," I said, "You two passed out. Get back to work."

"You officer?" asked Carla, pointing at me. I nodded and shunned the two cleaner ladies out of the elevator, rolling their carts along behind them.

"We have a shed to visit," I said as the doors closed, "But we need to stop by my house and get a few materials first."

"What are you talking about?" asked Sophia, "We've already done enough. Just let the stupid officers be. It's their own life they're putting in danger."

"You must be mad," I said, shaking my head, "We have to save them. The Cloaked One is going to be out there. Sheriff Morber is almost sure of it."

"Who cares what that oaf says?" asked Sophia, "The Cloaked One probably won't show up."

"I'm going," I said, "You might wanna hear my plan out before you start whining."

"Fine," said Sophia, hands on her hips, "What is it?"

"We have to be able to know where the Cloaked One went and what he did to the police," I said, "According to statistics, they know he'll be there tonight. Anyways, we have to get a bottle, cork, pin, and bright red food coloring."

"I see where you're going with this," said Sophia as we walked out of the elevator and hurried out of the building, "Go on."

"We fill up the bottle with red food coloring," I said, wheezing, "We put a pin in at the bottom to make sure the food coloring can come out, and then stop it with a cork. We need rope, as well, to attach the bottle to the underbelly of the cart. They're going somewhere at night. We attach the bottle right before they go, so too much food coloring isn't wasted."

"Genius," said Sophia, thumping me on the back, "Once we get everything prepared and explain our plan to everybody else, I think it'll be time to go."

I nodded, feeling pride swell up inside of me. It almost seemed as if a profound hole in the pit of my stomach was slowly being filled in. When Sophia and I got back to my house, we found Cerise and Carly playing a game of Spot It downstairs. They dropped the cards when we came in.

"Where the heck were you guys?" asked Carly, "We started to get worried."

"Police station," I panted, and Sophia and I filled Cerise and Carly in on what had happened and what we were planning to do.

"I feel well enough to go," said Cerise, standing up, "The doctor said my immune system is battling off the infection rather quickly, so I wanna go, too."

"I'm done for tonight," said Sophia, collapsing on the couch, "It's a genius plan and all, but I think I gotta rest."

"Okay," I said, tightening my grip around Cerise's hand, "Tell Bella, Ella, and Shella to come over. Our best hope is that the Cloaked One doesn't even show up. If he *does*, our best hope is that he kills nobody."

"Knowing the Cloaked One, that probably won't happen," said Sophia, massaging her aching muscles, "Let's just hope he kills only the people with a connection to the Black Sisterhood. And let's hope there *is* nobody there with a connection to the Black Sisterhood."

"Fair enough," I said, and turned to Cerise with a smile, "We have to get ready."

"You're really brave, Lex," she said, putting her head on my shoulder, "Really brave." I stroked her hair, taking in the scent of cinnamon and honey wafting from her.

"You guys get ready," said Carly, "We'll tell Bella, Ella, and Shella what's going on."

"Thanks," I said, squeezing Carly into a tight hug. I didn't let go for at least three minutes, tears forming in my eyes. Cerise cleared her throat and I finally withdrew myself, quickly blinking back the tears.

"You ready?" asked Cerise. I nodded and we headed to the garage to gather all the supplies.

I had a box filled with pins and corks in the garage which we gratefully used. Cerise dug through the recycling bin to find an empty water bottle and I collected rope and red food coloring.

We filled the bottle with the vivid food coloring and put the pin in. A stream of food coloring spilled from the bottle, and I high fived Cerise. It had worked. We put the cork in to stop the flow and I stuffed the rope into my pocket.

When we headed back inside, the whole Black Sisterhood was already gathered there. Bella was biting her fingernails nervously, Ella's eyes were strangely bright, and Shella looked extremely anxious.

Sophia was shaking her head. She looked around as we came in and said: "They think the plan's great, but are worried for you guys. They don't want the Cloaked One to get you, too."

"We'll be fine," said Cerise, extracting a Glock 36 from a small bag slung around her right shoulder, "If he runs away, we're in no harm. If he doesn't, we'll unmask him."

"I have to go to the bathroom," mumbled Shella and ran away. We heard the door close and her vomit all over the floor.

"Poor thing," said Ella, shaking her head, "I'll go check on her." Ella knocked on the door, but was met by another vicious vomiting sound.

"Come in," a weak voice croaked from inside, and Ella opened the door. I turned back to Sophia, Bella, Cerise, and Carly.

"Cerise and I have to go," I said, "We can't take too long, or they'll be off soon. We can't linger behind the cart as they're going, so we'll wait an hour in the police station shed. Then, we'll follow the red traces. If we're not back by midnight, come looking for us."

"Godspeed, guys," said Sophia in a shaky voice. Carly saluted us and Bella smiled edgily.

I turned to the door, clutching Cerise's hand for dear life. Maybe I wouldn't come back here tonight. Maybe the Cloaked One would get to me first...

CHAPTER THIRTEEN

When we made it to the police station, darkness was already eating away at the light sky. Cerise, who appeared to be quite high-strung at the moment, stood off to the side while I attached the bottle.

"Someone's coming!" hissed Cerise, and dove behind a box filled with guns.

I took this as cue to start tying the bottle onto the cart. Five officers, one of whom I recognized as Officer Wilkins, walked into the shed. They all looked ruddy-faced and were talking in hushed voices.

The officers collected some guns from the box Cerise was hiding behind, and clambered into the cart. They lowered the guns into satchels and Officer Wilkins started up the car, just as I finished tying the bottle.

As they were pulling away through the ajar doors, I removed the cork from the bottle. Food coloring poured out from inside, creating a trail behind them as they left the shed.

"Nice," whispered Cerise.

"Now we just have to wait an hour," I said, and Cerise cuddled up next to me.

The hour passed quickly, my heart beating faster and faster by the moment. Cerise lifted her head from my lap when there was five minutes to go. A spine-chilling scream had risen from the depths of the forest.

"Oh no," I uttered, and Cerise and I sprung to our feet. We began following the trail, quiet as mice, but filled with epinephrine. The night was dark and loomed upon us. The moon was our tour guide, reflecting off of the red trail, allowing us to continue our sprint.

As we went deeper into the woods, the trail was less visible. My neck ached from bending my head so much, but whenever I looked up to stretch it, I tripped over branches or brambles.

A light moan caught my attention and I stopped running. I turned around to find Cerise sprawled out on the ground.

"Cerise!" I cried, running over to help her. Her face was covered in dirt and a deep scratch ran through her leg.

"I'll be fine," she groaned, got up, and continued running. I followed after her, but stumbled on the way. I tasted blood and dirt, and felt a sharp pain in my ankle.

"Lex, c'mon!" yelled Cerise, and I rose to my feet. Cerise and I continued following the red trail for what seemed like an eternity. Another bloodcurdling scream came from an area very close to us.

"It's done," gasped Cerise in front of me. I looked up ahead. The red trail cut short where the cart had swerved to the side. I plummeted behind a tree, dragging Cerise behind me. My blood turned to ice as I looked at what had happened.

The Cloaked One was standing by a tree, holding a gun and a bloody knife. Two officers were cowering by a bush, but the Cloaked One wasn't coming for them. Officer Wilkins was pinned to a tree with the help of several knives. He was clearly dead. I stifled a scream. Two other officers were lying on the floor with bullet wounds in their heads and chests.

"Why isn't the Cloaked One coming for the other two?" asked Cerise.

"Isn't it obvious?" I mouthed back, making the slightest of sounds, "He's playing by his word. Those three must somehow be connected to the Black Sisterhood."

"Oh God!" suddenly cried Cerise, pointing at one dead man on the ground, "I've met that guy before! He and Ella's father used to work together, but they're still close friends. That is, were."

I whimpered in terror, "Officer Wilkins has a very close connection to Sheriff Morber who has a close connection to us," I said.

"What about the other guy?" asked Cerise, and I shrugged in reply.

"What're we doing?" I suddenly said in a shrill voice, "Let's go after the Cloaked One!"

I noticed the Cloaked One hauling a moving bag behind him. A head popped out from the opening, but the Cloaked One forced it back down. I recognized the head. It was Hildred.

"Stop moving!" snarled the Cloaked One in a strident, masculine voice. He withdrew a gun from the depths of his cloak and shot the man in the head. I heard Hildred shriek, and saw his hand shoot up to clutch his head in agony.

"Hildred," said Cerise, and crumpled to the ground. She sobbed quietly, but I lifted her back to her feet.

"Perfect time to unmask him," I said, "He can't run too fast while hauling the dead body of a man behind him. Let's go."

The Cloaked One, as expected, was elusive. He swerved in and out of trees, desperate to escape the scene. I doubted he knew we were behind him, which gave us an even greater advantage.

Just as we were getting ever so close to catching him, he dove away and disappeared from sight. Cerise kicked a tree angrily, and I clutched my face. We had lost him again.

"Let's go back to the men," said Cerise, "Best we can do right now." I agreed and Cerise and I made our way back to the clearing. The two men were still cowering behind the bush.

"You're safe," I said in a voice very unlike my own, "You can go now."

"Who are you?" asked one of the officers, looking even more intimidated.

"Black Sisterhood members," pronounced Cerise, and helped the two officers up, "Trust us, you're good to go. Go to Sheriff Morber's office and tell him what happened."

"Thank you," said one of officers, grasping onto a tree. He looked inordinately green and sweaty. His fellow looked slightly worse, but managed to drag his feet along behind the other man.

"Sheriff Morber'll handle everything," said Cerise, a slight tone of sharpness in her voice, "Suppose he's our only hope now. C'mon, we can't leave the dead bodies here."

"No, we have to," I snapped, "If Sheriff Morber finds three dead bodies in our house, do you know how much attention we'll attract?"

Cerise sharply inhaled, but let the matter go, "Well, we have to at least take pictures," she said, "Then we'll go back home."

A growing knot of tension and unease was forming in my stomach. I watched as Cerise went to every dead body, snapping pictures. As she was taking a picture of the unknown man, his hand shot up and grabbed her knee.

Cerise squealed in fright, and jumped back. The man moaned, still holding on to Cerise's knee.

"T-the Cloaked One didn't kill you?" she stuttered. I gazed at the man, thunderstruck. He pulled back his hair, revealing a necklace tied around his forehead. The bullet had gone into the center of the necklace, saving the man's life.

I helped the man up, and he coughed out some blood. Cerise grabbed the man's legs and I took his arms. We managed to carry him all the way back home, stopping occasionally for breaks.

"Did he get you in the chest?" I asked, my fear slowly ebbing away. The man pulled his shirt up, revealing an intense wound. I gasped and Cerise and I hurried to get him to the door.

"Open the door!" yelled Cerise loudly, and Carly swung open the door. Her face turned ghostly pale as we carried the bleeding, weak officer inside.

"What the hell happened?" asked Sophia as we gently placed the man on the couch. Mom hurried into the living room, looking horror-struck.

"Get help!" I said in an intrusive voice. Mom rushed up to her room to get supplies. She came back down, still lost for words. Carly and Mom helped remove the bullet from the man's chest as he wheezed in pain. Every breath seemed to be getting harder and harder for him.

"Tell them what happened," I said, nodding in Cerise's direction. I began to apply pressure on the cut and clean the wound out.

"Get antibiotic cream!" screeched Mom, and Carly ran upstairs to the medicine cabinet.

Sophia, Bella, Ella, and Shella sat in astounded silence. Ella buried her face in her hands at the mention of the man her father had known. Sophia began to cry when Cerise told them about Hildred being shot in the bag.

"What a shame," said Bella, fiddling with her necklace, "What a shame you guys couldn't catch up to the Cloaked One."

As Carly, Mom, and I tended to the injured man, Cerise retreated to the guest bedroom to rest. Sophia soon bid us goodnight and left, followed by everyone else.

Exhaustion pressed in on me, but I refused to give in. The man had drifted off to sleep, and his breathing was becoming steadier. Mom gently continued to treat his bullet wound. Carly dozed off on the couch, curling up into a ball.

"Go to bed, Lex," said Mom, her face wrinkled in fatigue, "He'll be better by tomorrow morning."

"It's okay," I said, "I'm not too tired." I could feel my hands trembling and my brain begging me to rest, but the man needed help.

"No, Alexis, I mean it," said Mom. Her tone of voice was stony and demanding, but her eyes were rumpled in kindness.

"Okay," I said, and leaned over to kiss Mom, "Good night."

The night was restless and uncalm for me. I drifted off to sleep, but only for short periods of time. Nightmares filled my head. Flashbacks of the Cloaked One shooting Hildred, flashbacks of Officer Wilkins pinned to the tree, flashbacks of the man clutching Cerise's knee in despair.

When I awoke, I heard a commotion in the kitchen. An unfamiliar voice drifted up the staircase, and the scent of pancakes cleared the sleepiness out of my head.

My hair a disheveled mess, I made my way down the steps. The world was swaying around me, and my limbs ached with debility. The wounded officer was lying underneath a blanket, talking to Sophia. He looked much better, but still weak.

Carly continued to clear his wound, injecting charcoal up his nose to neutralize the lead in his stomach. Sophia and the man were sharing jokes, smiling and laughing. A platter of Mom's infamous pancakes lay on the table beside them.

"Hi," I said, not knowing how to say what was on my mind, "How's everything with you?"

"I'm doing fantastic," replied the man, "God bless you and your Mom. Would've rotted on the ground without ya."

I fought the question I so desperately wanted to ask from bubbling up to the surface. Forcing a tight smile, I took a pancake from the platter.

"Lex, what's up?" asked Sophia, "You look constipated. Do you want to ask something?"

"What happened last night out in the forest?" I asked, feeling like a jar whose contents had been spilled.

The man went quiet and Sophia cleared her throat. I heard a shuffle of feet behind me, and turned around to find the rest of the Black Sisterhood coming in.

"Well," began the man, "You saved my life, after all. I suppose it wouldn't hurt you to know. But you gotta tell me a couple things first. How'd you know where we were?"

"We found out you guys were going," I said, folding my arms, "We then attached a bottle with red food coloring to the underbelly of the cart, and followed the trail the food coloring left behind."

"Wow," said the officer, "Before I begin, my name's Hugo. Nice to meet you, Lexie."

"I told him your name," said Sophia, giggling. As I leaned in to shake Hugo's hand, I was surprised by how young he was. Hugo seemed to be only a couple years older than me, with his bright blue eyes and black hair.

"How old are you?" I asked, sitting on the couch.

"Seventeen," responded Hugo, "I joined the police officers not long ago. They nominated me to go to the forest, considering I was one of the most inexperienced ones."

"Cruel," I mumbled, "That's horrific. How did you know to tie that necklace around your head?"

"I consider that necklace good luck," replied Hugo, "All of the police officers think it's ugly and foolish, so I tied it out of sight."

"Well, it saved your life," I said, "Can you tell me what happened in the forest?"

"A deal's a deal, I suppose," said Hugo, wrapping his blanket tighter around him, "When I got in the cart, I was more nervous than ever. We saw the Cloaked One lingering in the trees and began to follow him. I huddled in the back, too afraid to do anything. When we got closer to the Cloaked One, he suddenly stopped in the place you found me.

"Officer Wilkins got out first and aimed to shoot the Cloaked One. Too bad for him, the Cloaked One was quick. Got a couple knives out of his cloak and pinned the guy to the tree. All of us got scared, and huddled down in the cart. Officer Barnes was next to get killed."

"Officer Barnes," muttered Ella, sniffling slightly, "He was a great man."

"Officer Jones and Officer Brown were on top of me," continued Hugo, "I thought I was safe. What surprised me was that the Cloaked One didn't even attempt to kill Officer Jones and Officer Brown. He just threw them to the side. When he saw me, he shot me twice and threw me out of the cart. After that, he just stood there. Then you guys came along and saved me."

"Oh my God," said Sophia, "I know why Officer Jones and Officer Brown weren't killed."

"Please do tell me," said Hugo sarcastically, "That way I can avoid being shot next time."

"It's unavoidable," said Shella, "The Cloaked One comes after everyone with a connection to the Black Sisterhood. We don't know why, though."

"The Black Sisterhood?" said Hugo in an insipid tone, "Never heard of it. Are you two members?"

"Yeah, we all are," I said, "Do you know anyone named Sophia Persefoni?"

"No," said Hugo thoughtfully, "But my grandfather knew someone named Amanda Persefoni."

"That was my great aunt's name," said Sophia, quivering like a leaf in brutal autumn winds, "How does the Cloaked One know all this?"

"His helper," said Bella, "Remember that note you got? The one you told us all about? The Cloaked

One and his helper must be close to the Black Sisterhood themselves."

"I think it was the real Cloaked One last night," said Cerise, "The note said that the Cloaked One's helper did everything unwillingly. The Cloaked One's helper doesn't actually want to kill, but is being threatened. The Cloaked One last night really seemed to enjoy killing."

"I agree with Cerise," I said, "I think it was the actual Cloaked One in action yesterday. It really seemed like it."

"Right," said Hugo, "You guys seem to know a lot. Are you detectives or somethin'?"

"Sorta," I said. The loud ring of the doorbell echoed through the house, startling me. Hugo curled up underneath his blanket and dozed off. Carly moistened his forehead and lips, looking debilitated.

"I got it," said Sophia, but I trailed behind her as she went to open the door. A man stood behind it, looking jumpy. Sophia opened the door, and shock fell upon me.

It was the man from last night. The man who we had sent to Sheriff Morber's office.

"May I come in?" asked the man, "My name is Officer Jones. My fellow, Officer Brown, isn't feeling well so he couldn't make it. We'd like to thank you once more for scaring the Cloaked One away."

"That wasn't us," said Sophia, closing the door behind Officer Jones, "What did Sheriff Morber say?"

The old man's face fell and he put a hand on Sophia's shoulder. I glanced behind us, where Cerise, Bella, Ella, and Shella stood. Curiosity shone on their faces and I looked back at Officer Jones.

"This is Officer Jones," I said, addressing the Black Sisterhood, "He has news about what Sheriff Morber said."

"I have to go," said Shella, checking her phone, "Charlie's getting worried."

"Don't go back to that sicko," said Bella, holding her back. Shella shook her head and pushed past.

"I really have to," she said, "My parents have a close relationship with Charlie, and I don't want to get in trouble."

"Don't you want to hear what Officer Jones has to say?" asked Sophia, grabbing Shella by the shoulder.

"You can text me about it later," said Shella, "Bye, guys." She pushed open the door and walked out. I glared at Officer Jones suspiciously.

"How'd you find my house?" I asked defensively.

"You told me you're a Black Sisterhood member," answered Officer Jones, "There's a whole section for the Black Sisterhood in the Parkersburg phonebook. Your addresses are there, too. I traveled to every one of your houses, but this was the only one with people."

"Was Charlie in Shella's house?" I asked.

"I don't know who that is," said Officer Jones, "I rang the doorbell to Shella's house, but nobody answered. He might've been in there for all I know."

"Anyways," interrupted Ella, "What's the news? What's wrong?"

"Officer Brown got terribly sick on the way," began Officer Jones, "I told him to go back home. After I made sure he was alright, I proceeded to Sheriff Morber's office. Sheriff Morber wasn't there. I started to get worried, thinking that he had gotten hurt."

"Did he show up?" I asked, dreading what Officer Jones was going to say next.

"Yes," said Officer Jones, "But he was in horrible conditions. He was covered in sweat and fresh blood, all over him. The poor guy looked like he had run ten miles without breaking."

"So, what are you insinuating?" asked Sophia, her eyebrows knit with perplexion.

Officer Jones took a deep breath before telling us: "Ladies, I have been an officer for more than forty years. And I think that Sheriff Morber may be the Cloaked One."

A deathly silence followed the officer's last statement. We all were too scared to admit that he might've been right.

CHAPTER FOURTEEN

"Thank you, Officer Jones," said Sophia, looking very neurotic, "We'll investigate further." "He killed Hugo!" sobbed Officer Jones, "So young and so reckless."

"It's okay, Officer Jones," I said, "Hugo is in my living room. We saved him and he's already feeling much better. Only one bullet got him, and the wound wasn't too bad."

"Oh, thank God," said Officer Jones, "Well, I'll leave you girls to it. Have a nice day!"

"Bye, Officer," mumbled Cerise, and slammed the door behind Officer Jones as he walked out.

"We have to go tonight," said Ella, turning towards me, "Forget Tuesday. We have to go tonight."

"Ella's right," said Bella, "Officer Jones has a point. It may very well be Sheriff Morber. But who would the helper be?"

"It could be anyone," I said, shrugging, "Ella and I will go to the House of Doom tonight. We'll catch the Cloaked One once and for all."

"Someone should check on Shella first," said Sophia, "I'm worried about her."

"I'll go," said Cerise, "Lex can come with me."

"Lex already has enough on her plate," said Bella, "I'll come with you, Cerise."

"Sure," I said, "That's fine by me. I think I'm going to sleep a bit more."

"Sweet dreams," said Sophia sardonically, "Don't come down too late, Sleeping Beauty. Oh, oops, I mean Sleeping Ugliness."

I laughed and shoved Sophia in the shoulder playfully. Cerise and Bella slipped away, and I watched them head to Shella's house. Ella and Sophia joined Carly in the living room. Carly was feeding Hugo as much food as possible, for he needed to regain strength.

I walked up the stairs, leaning onto the railing. The world felt so unreal and I pressed my head against the cool surface of the wall to calm down. Everything seemed to sway and my head pounded.

"Lexie?" I heard Mom say, "Are you okay?" It sounded as if she was calling through a tunnel, miles away from me, somewhere underwater.

I felt her strong, warm hands under my armpits, lifting me up. She carried me all the way to bed, and tucked me underneath the blanket.

"Sleep," I heard her say. The world grew dark, foggy, and lonely and I soon found myself in a vacuum of blackness.

An evil, cold voice filled the void. I saw Sophia and Cerise floating by me, both dead. A cloaked figure was hovering over me, seeming to take up all of the endless space.

"Little heroes always die," the cloaked figure said, and cackled. I felt inexplicable pain as the thing removed a gun from its boundless cloak and shot me in the head.

"They always die," repeated the voice, and I felt my heart pound out of my chest and my body slump in unconsciousness. I wasn't alive, but I sensed it. I sensed the pressure on me, the continuous screaming for help, the feeling that everything was wrong. Including me.

I woke to a shrill scream erupting from my throat. Sophia was leaning by my bedside, holding a cup of chamomile tea.

"Lex!" she cried, "What's going on?" Sophia thrust the cup into my hands and I drank gratefully.

"Bad dream," I panted, wiping a stream of cold sweat from my forehead, "Thanks for the tea."

"Sure," said Sophia, standing up and stretching, "Cerise and Bella are back. They've got quite the story."

"What is it?" I asked, standing up. The world swayed for a moment, but quickly went back to normal. My knees buckled, and I collapsed to the floor.

"Maybe you should skip on the House of Doom tonight," said Sophia, "I can go with Ella."

"No," I said, groaning and leaning on Sophia for support, "I'll be fine. It isn't that big of a deal."

"Okay," said Sophia, and heaved me off of her, "Do something with that hair of yours and come down."

I stumbled downstairs, running a wet comb through my hair. Nausea erupted through my body, but I refused to give in to it. Cerise and Bella were sitting on the couch, retelling what they had seen at Shella's house.

"Hey," I said, and Cerise ran up to me. She squeezed me into a hug, and I fought the urge to peel her off of me. Some kind of anger towards her boiled inside of me.

"What happened at Shella's?" I asked, casually pushing Cerise away. Ella shook her head, looking prostrated.

"Shella isn't well, I'm afraid," began Bella, "When we walked in, Charlie was scolding her for climbing up a tall tree and falling off. Shella looked horrible. She had a broken leg, sprained wrist, and hundreds of bruises and scratches."

"We asked if Shella could come back to Lex's place," added Cerise, "Charlie said that she was grounded. Poor thing."

"She never should've gone up that tree in the first place," I grumbled, and Sophia rolled her eyes exasperatedly.

"No, Lex is right," retorted Ella, "What kind of demons would chase Shella up that tree? Why would she have gone up that tree and involuntarily fallen off? Something's fishy."

"It is, indeed," said a singsong voice behind us. Mom and Carly were carrying platters of tuna sandwiches into the room. I held my nose in disgust.

The day seemed to stretch on forever. Carly took care of Hugo as Ella paced around the house, mentally preparing herself for the House of Doom. Bella played a game of chess with Sophia, while Cerise begged me to take a walk with her.

"Not today," I snapped, and headed up to my room, "I'm not in the mood." With that, I slammed the door shut in Cerise's face. A slight twinge of guilt burned inside of me, but I pushed it away. I didn't know what was going on.

When night had fallen, Ella and I were ready. We both were dressed in black and had taken a page out of Hugo's book, tying necklaces around our foreheads.

Ella carried five daggers, tucked away into the black belt tied around her waist. I carried two guns in a light satchel draped over my shoulders.

When I came down, Sophia and Ella were steadily arguing about something. Cerise lay on the couch, curling her hair with a pencil. Bella sat on a chair, back rigid, watching the argument as if it were a tennis match.

"Ella, stop being ridiculous!" cried Sophia, "You don't need that many daggers, c'mon! It's a waste of supplies!"

"Well, try to be brave when you're about to come face to face with the Cloaked One," snarled Ella, and beckoned for me to come down.

"Bye, guys," I said softly, and everyone waved. Sophia stood, fuming, her arms crossed. Her face broke into a smile when I looked at her.

Everything seemed to happen in slow motion as we approached the House of Doom. Ella kicked open the door, and we walked in. I swept some dust off the floor and sat down. Ella followed, and took a ham sandwich out of my satchel.

"Af foon af we fee the Cloaked Vun, we go," she said with a full mouth.

"I m sorry, I don t speak Latin. We have to follow him," I added, "It s a risk, but we overnumber him in weapons and in people."

Ella swallowed, and everything went still. I bounded up, followed by Ella who withdrew a dagger from her belt. We heard subdued footsteps outside, and rushed to the second floor.

"I see him!" suddenly cried Ella, making me jump about a mile high. I ran up to the window next to her, and blew the layers of dust off.

Sure enough, a cloaked figure stood by the house, looking up. I took a gun out of my satchel, and pushed Ella forward. We silently made our way downstairs, peeking out of windows to make sure we hadn t lost the Cloaked One.

"He s off," I whispered, pointing at the cloaked figure through the window. The Cloaked One had looked around briefly and then slipped away into the dark and treacherous forest.

"Go!" sputtered Ella, and I blasted down the front door. It broke into wooden splinters, as we ran over the wreckage and into the forest. The Cloaked One didn't stop to look around and kept sprinting through the trees.

Ella stumbled on a tree root but I grabbed her arm just in time. She groaned in pain as her leg hit a tree and blood gushed from the scratch it had caused.

We continued rocketing after the Cloaked One, pausing to quickly catch our breaths. Ella ran ahead of me, clutching a stitch in her side. She looked dog-tired, leaning against a tree, her eyes rolling back in her head.

"Drink!" I muttered, shoving a bottle of water into Ella s hands. She chugged it down, spilling water all over herself in the process. The Cloaked One had stopped to survey the forest, head tilted towards us.

"I-I-I can t do this anymore," said Ella, collapsing to the ground.

"Get up, you stupid couch potato!" I cried, fury rushing through me, "We haven t been running for that long!"

"Shut up," snarled Ella, allowing herself to be picked up from the ground. She wrapped her arms around my waist, and I began to run at a sedate pace. Her feet dragged along the ground, nails digging into my stomach.

"Just run!" I yelled, pushing Ella up. She floundered a few feet trying to regain control. Her breaths quick and sharp, Ella steadied herself and began to run again.

The trees grew closer together around us, giving me the feeling of being trapped. A wide grassy clearing stretched out beyond a circle of lofty trees. The Cloaked One stopped there and turned around. It lowered itself to the ground and twiddled the grass between its gloved fingers.

"This is some kind of trap," Ella wheezed, running up beside me, "Why did the Cloaked One stop running?"

I pressed my index finger to my lips and Ella fell silent. The Cloaked One rose to its feet lethargically, still idly fiddling with a strand of grass.

I raised my gun, aiming at the Cloaked One 's foot. Ella took out a dagger and threw it at a tree beside the Cloaked One. Its head snapped towards the dagger in confusion.

"Now, " mumbled Ella, and I squeezed the trigger. The Cloaked One dodged the bullet just in time, diving to the ground and rolling away.

I aimed my gun once more and pulled the trigger. The bullet tore through the Cloaked One 's boot, entering its skin. It cried in pain, though the gender was indistinguishable.

"Aim for the kill! " cried Ella, but was a bit too loud. The Cloaked One rose to its feet, swaying from side to side. It charged towards Ella, and Ella 's piercing scream filled the forest.

The Cloaked One sunk a dagger into Ella 's chest. I froze, horrified. Ella moaned in agony, crumpling to the ground. She pulled the bloody dagger out and threw it on the grass.

"ELLA! " I roared, kneeling beside Ella. Blood was oozing out of the dagger wound, and she was steadily going pale. Her hand shot up to squeeze mine.

Ella sobbed into my shoulder, and I put her head in my lap. Tears and blood were streaked all over her pallid face, and her eyes reflected sorrow and pain.

"Help, " she uttered, "Help. I don 't want to die!"

"We 'll get you out of here, " I said, grief burning inside of me, "I promise. "

Indescribable pain filled my insides. All happiness was squeezed out of my system as Ella 's head fell to the ground and her eyes fluttered shut.

My face wet and stinging with the wind, I grabbed a stick and swung at the Cloaked One.

It fell to the ground, defeated. I threw the stick away and grabbed Ella by the arms, throwing her over my shoulder. She was still breathing, but ever so slowly.

Soaked in Ella 's blood, I ripped the Cloaked One's cloak off. My heart rose into my throat, and I screamed. An owl hooted indignantly from above, but my focal point was secured on staying conscious and returning to my awaiting friends.

Grabbing the Cloaked One 's feeble body, I hauled the two back to the House of Doom. Affliction pressed at my chest and I sobbed into the growing night.

My hair was caked with sweat and tears. Streaks of blood and dirt shown on my face, and I felt tortured on the inside.

"HELP! " I screeched, my desolate voice cutting through the deathly silent night, "HELP! " Despondency crept into my soul and I heard the door of my house open.

Footsteps soon thundered the ground, making my migraine even worse. I threw the two bodies to the ground, and leaned onto Sophia for support.

"Ella! " sniveled Bella, "Ella 's dead! " Ella was no longer breathing. She lay unconscious on the ground, blood still seeping out of the dagger wound.

"The Cloaked One, " whispered Cerise, gazing down at the body next to Ella 's, "The Cloaked One's helper. I don 't believe it.

"Shella, " said Sophia. The very mention of Shella made goosebumps appear on my arms and legs.

"Yes, " I said, tears streaming down my face, "Shella is the Cloaked One 's helper."

CHAPTER FIFTEEN

A couple days later, Shella sat in Sheriff Morber's office. She was attached to a lie detector and looked brittle. Ella's funeral was being held the following day, and Sophia was busy helping with the preparations, assisted by Hugo.

Cerise, Bella, and I glared at Shella from across the room. Sheriff Morber sat in his chair, fingers together. He took out his notepad filled with questions and began to talk.

"Shella," he said, "Are you the Cloaked One's helper?"

"Yes, sir," said Shella, tears shining in her eyes, "Unwillingly."

"That I understand," said Sheriff Morber, "Who is the Cloaked One?"

Shella took a deep breath, "My cousin, Charlie, sir," she responded, and Bella gasped. Cerise let go of my hand, and pressed her head against the bulletin board.

"Did you murder Roberto and Olga?"

"No, sir."

"Alexis's father?"

"No, sir."

"Dillon and Albert?"

"Yes, sir."

"Ella?"

"Yes, sir."

"I suppose everyone else?" asked Sheriff Morber.

"Yes, sir," responded Shella, looking guilty, "Against my will. Charlie hurt me. Everyone but the officers in the forest. That was Charlie."

"Were you really sick on the night of the murder of Archer's family?" questioned Sheriff Morber.

"No, sir," said Shella.

"How has Charlie hurt you before?" asked Sheriff Morber.

"I was the one who sent the Black Sisterhood the letter saying that the Cloaked One had a helper," said Shella, "Charlie was really holding my family captive and threatening me and them if I didn't fulfill the tasks. When Charlie found out that I had sent that letter, he threw me off of a tree. I didn't really fall off."

I felt my heart pound melodies of fear against my ribcage as Cerise whimpered.

"Do you know why Charlie did this? Do you know who killed the family thirty years ago?" asked Sheriff Morber.

"Yes, sir," said Shella, "Charlie told me. His grandfather killed the family. That family was blood relatives of Sophia's grandmother through unknown causes. Sophia's grandmother was thinking about starting a small gang, but thought Sophia was best for the job."

"Why kill everyone related to the Black Sisterhood?" asked the Sheriff.

"Charlie's grandpa believed that anyone connected to the Black Sisterhood is a threat," said Shella, "Charlie made me join the Black Sisterhood so I wouldn't seem like a suspect. I didn't want to join, sir."

"Holy cow," said Cerise, her knees mangling, "Holy cow."

"So Charlie's sick grandfather passed on that belief to Charlie?" asked Sheriff Morber.

"Yes, sir," said Shella. She was trembling from head to toe.

"Who looks up at the House of Doom every night?" I blurted out, unable to control myself.

"Charlie," replied Shella, refusing to make eye contact with me, "He's the bad guy here."

"Were Keisha Allens and Tim Roberts somehow related to the Black Sisterhood?" asked Sheriff Morber.

"No, sir," said Shella, her bottom lip quivering, "It was just a beginning to scare the Black Sisterhood. Charlie made me drown and strangle them."

"Shella," I murmured, and Shella bent her head down, "Who are Braveheart and Merciless?"

"My parents," said Shella, a tear slipping from her half-closed eyes, "You heard that night, didn't you? You heard when I said my parents would hear about that, but then Charlie took them from me."

"Yeah," I said, taking a seat on a chair facing Shella, "I saw you with him only two nights. The rest, he was alone."

"That's after he found out you lived in the house across from our meeting place," explained Shella, "Before, he, I guess you could say, trained me for the tasks ahead. The tasks of murdering. I don't know if you saw *this*, but Charlie made me throw knives at trees every night. He trained me with a gun normally on weekends."

"I see," I said, "That's why he once told you you weren't doing something right. But, Shella, the night you guys talked about Braveheart and Merciless, what did you mean by him circling you and preying upon you like a hawk?"

"The night I completed Task Five," said Shella in a hoarse, quivering voice, "Charlie was looking at me the entire time, hidden behind a closet. At home, he told me about his schemes, his hideout, and how he planned to use me."

"That's terrible," I muttered, wiping a runaway tear from my cheek, "That's cruel of Charlie. I hope he has something to say for himself at the funeral."

"You know," began Shella, a myriad of tears flowing down her cheeks, "I'm here right now, because of my love for the Black Sisterhood. Charlie and I would still be on the loose, committing crimes, if not for my love for Ella. As soon as I killed her upon Charlie's orders, I knew there was no way I could continue the crimes that had destroyed my life."

"You will face court time and jail shortly," said Sheriff Morber, seeming quite uninterested in Shella's fate as he breathed in the fetid fumes of a cigarette.

"Sir, no!" cried Shella, "You don't understand."

"I do," said Sheriff Morber, "You may go to Ella's funeral tomorrow if you want to. Case closed."

Bella hurried up to Shella as Sheriff Morber left the office. Shella was crumpled over, sobbing into her hands.

"Hey," said Bella, "It's okay. Hey, listen to me."

"I'm a murderer!" cried Shella, looking at Bella with miserable eyes, "Once a murderer, always a murderer."

"That may be true," began Bella, "But you have to come to Ella's funeral tomorrow."

"You're right, huh?" said Shella sarcastically, "The murderer coming to the person's funeral."

Tears gushed down Bella's face and she sniffled, "It's what Ella would've wanted," said Bella, "She'd want you to come. She'd want you to be there for her."

"I'm the reason she's lying in that coffin!" sobbed Shella.

"Maybe," said Bella, "But Ella and I will love you forever. Please come tomorrow."

"Okay," said Shella, grasping Bella's hands, "Just as long as you promise to visit me. In j-jail."

"Once a friend, always a friend," said Bella, and hugged Shella tightly. Shella cried into her shoulder as Bella soothed her, tears of her own falling into Shella's hair.

I knew I'd never forget that moment. Never forget the kindness Bella showed that day as she hugged and consoled the person who had killed so many.

"I'm sorry it had to end this way," murmured Bella, as we left to help Sophia and Hugo with the funeral preparations.

Fog encapsulated everything. Rain came down in torrents from the sky, and thunder rumbled menacingly. Ella's funeral was held in a vast room with high ceilings. She lay in a casket on a stage surrounded by velvet red curtains.

Shella, Cerise, Sophia, Bella, and I all stood by the stage wearing black robes. Ella's casket was open, revealing her. She had been dressed in a beautiful white gown and was clutching a flower close to her heart.

Sophia wept into her robe, stroking Ella's hair. Ella's mother and father sat at a table close to the stage, blowing their noses and bawling. Hugo, Mom, and Carly were also at a table near the stage.

Ella's mother gave a speech that shattered my heart to pieces. I watched as she came up to Ella and placed a bouquet of roses in her pallid hands.

"I love you," wept Ella's mother, "Dad and I love you more than anything. Betrayal happened to you, I'm afraid. Betrayal by someone you held dear. But God will take you back home, dear Ella. May you rest in peace."

One by one, each member of the Black Sisterhood came to pay their respects to Ella. Bella knelt by her and delicately put a flower crown into her hair.

"Loved by all," she began, clasping her hands together and letting a few tears fall free, "Respected by all. Cared for by all. Envied by all. Ella, God Bless You in your journey ahead. In your journey to heaven."

Cerise was next, heaving sobs and stroking Ella's dress, "You have always led me through darkness and light. Through day and night. Soon, you will spread your wings and take flight to the heavens. I love you, Ella. I will miss you," said Cerise, and showered Ella with rose petals.

"The last words I said to you," sobbed Sophia, kneeling by Ella, "Were cruel. Ella, I never meant for it to end this way. I'll talk to you everyday. You're someone I look up to. You deserve only the best. I love you."

Shella took a deep breath and walked forward. She was met by a chorus of "boos" and Ella's mother screaming at her to step away.

Shella did something nobody expected her to do. She touched Ella in the spot where she had been stabbed. Everyone gasped and yelled.

"It's all my fault," said Shella, "Everything. You lying in this casket, us being here, everyone crying... I love you more than anything else in this world. You are my light, my joy, and my everything. I think I know why I killed you. I killed you because God was so desperately begging for you to come home. That's where you belong. In heaven with all the angels. Ella, *you* are my guardian angel. Rest in peace."

As Shella made her way back, everyone applauded. I patted Shella on the back as she howled mournfully.

I slowly made my way to Ella, my fingers sweaty from clutching the flower so tightly. I knelt by her, a lump forming in my throat.

"I don't want to die," I began, "Those were the last words you said. I promised to you that I would get you back safely. I lied. I broke my promise. I'm sorry. Ella, I never got to properly say goodbye. But I won't need to say goodbye, because I know that you'll always be with the Black Sisterhood. In mind, in soul, in heart, and in spirit. Rest in peace."

A sob came from the audience. I turned around to find Charlie standing by the stage, covered in tears. Everyone gasped as Charlie came up to Ella and placed three roses into her hands. He struggled to speak, continuing to cry.

"I'm a cold-blooded monster," began the murderer, "Every morsel within me bears remorse for what I imposed upon so many innocent families in this town. Ella is not the only one whose soul was brought to the ethers due to my brutality. With utter sincerity, I apologize for my actions. Over my life, I pined to abstain from the direly horrid deeds my grandfather indulged in. However, the benign part of me was overtaken by something macabre, something malicious, and doings unforgivable by the kindest. For what it is worth, I'm sorry. May the victims rest in peace."

Charlie was met with a very cautious, yet steadfast, applause from the audiences. A flaxen harmony of tears and blessings rose from the persons situated within the seats facing Ella's coffin.

Although this was indefinitely my imagination, it was ever so lovely to perceive the ghost of Ella rising from its resting spot and surveying the crowd with a smile of despondency, yet such profound amiability. Ella's eyes meandered upon her guests and fixated rather stolidly upon Stella and Charlie, who stood in the front row, entirely disregarding one another's existence.

"Don't be infuriated at the two," I whispered, and the former Black Sisterhood member glanced at me. "No, they are not indigenous to the land of callous habits. They are simply misled. Mistaken.

They are not bad children. There is no such thing. They are merely youngsters endeavoring to battle through the currents of life's hardships. Their actions are unpardonable, but I'm afraid we shall have to muster all courage within us and release the grudges. We love you, Ella, and that shall always be a credence endemic to us. Do not dwell upon the misery of leaving us, for you are always welcome to visit. I do not tinker with the metaphysical, but you, I suppose, can pass as an exception."

I was hardly aware of these words eluding my mind, but they seemed to register quite well with the abstract form of Ella. Without further ado, the ghost doused herself with an air of remission and planted a kiss atop Shella's quavering cheek.

"She's beautiful," muttered Cerise, approaching me, her glassy eyes fixed on the wavering spirit of Ella.

"Indeed," I responded, entwining my fingers within Cerise's tremulous ones. "Hey, relax. Everything will be alright. Life goes on, despite the blemishes of distress. Do not afflict yourself. Enjoy this. It is not everyday that you discern such a wondrous happening. Although Ella herself may be long gone, her energy inhabits us perennially. And that, can be attested to by the vision forth our eyes."

"No matter what happens next," enunciated Cerise, steadying her fingers within my own. "We'll be ready. And we don't fight out of the sheer urge for fame, money, or other trivial matters. We fight out of love for each other. I presume that how it shall always be. Promise me one thing, Lex. Come what may, we will never forget each other. Or the Black Sisterhood. Promise."

"Cerise, you can forever entrust me with that aspiration," I answered, blinking away at the tears my emotions gleaned so effortlessly. "The Black Sisterhood wholly changed my life. In some instances, I wish I had never joined. Most of the time, however, I am so grateful to have met you guys. I don't know what I would do without you. This entirely new way of life is so peculiar to me, but it is teeming with thrill, love, tears, and so many adventures that will not be disparaged in the future. Oh, but I assume all wonderful friendships start with venturing through animosity's uncharted waters. I love you all. I know that nothing can break us apart. Here's to more memories."

"Here's to more memories," Cerise repeated in turn, entangling her pinkie finger within mine. Although Sophia, Bella, and even Shella were across the room, I could almost sense their promises ringing within our circle of trust. And although Ella had fallen to the "enemy", the fruitful quintessence of her heart would forever beat melodies of love within our coterie of faith...